My

Sister's

Funeral

www.cyberworldpublishing.com

This book is copyright © Stephen Bush 2011
First published by Cyberworld Publishing in 2011
Cover photo © Stephanie Swartz | Dreamstime.com
Cover Design S Bush

National Library of Australia Cataloguing-in-Publication entry
Bush, Stephen, 1953-
My sister's funeral : a murder mystery / by Stephen Bush.
ISBN:9781921879722 (pbk.)
Dewey Number: A823.4

Published by Cyberworld Publishing, Jindalee St, Toronto NSW
Australia

My
Sister's Funeral

Stephen Bush

CHAPTER 1

My sister disappeared on the 17th of September 1973.

Over thirty years ago.

I was ten when Maria went missing. Now I am a grown man, and I've been married and divorced, and a lot has changed in the world. When she went missing, Australians were still fighting in Vietnam. No one had heard of the mobile phone yet, and no one had a computer in their home. Hard to imagine.

I was ten. I know that. How could I forget? It isn't that I remember because I missed her so much, I can admit now that I hardly knew her. How well do most ten-year-old boys know a seventeen-year-old sister? Not very well, I'm sure.

No. I remember because of what went afterwards. Because from the first night she failed to come home from school, my childhood was over. It hadn't been a particularly wonderful childhood, but it hadn't been too bad either, and it was certainly better before she disappeared than it was after.

Since then the world has changed without missing her at all, and my world changed completely because of her. And it changed in many ways, including ways I'd rather not discuss with anyone. Because in one way especially she had never completely gone and had become an ever-more-important part of my life.

And now that I know who killed her?

There is no such thing as closure—only an unending parade of memories, open wounds, and the need to get on with living and to forget. I think perhaps it would have been better if she had never been found. If she had remained where she had been hidden, until she was part of the soil and recycled into the endless flow of the seasons, of birth, life, and death.

If there were to be closure for me I had thought that it would come, appropriately, on the day of her funeral. In a way it did.

I have visited her grave once since, but I still didn't feel closure or sorrow, what I felt was more a deep sadness, and yes, anger. Anger that in her short life she was such a catalyst for destruction.

Even her funeral had been no different.

* * * *

"I'm early," I said loudly to the woman arranging flowers in the memorial chapel. "Is Keith around?"

The funeral was being held in the large chapel at the Cylore cemetery, so the venue was a neutral one. But the minister from the local Anglican church would be conducting the service. We had never been a religious family, but my mother, Amelia, had turned fervently to various religions in the years after Maria disappeared.

The minister had been around long enough to have listened to my mother at some time when the Anglican Church had been in favor with her. So he knew us, or about us anyway, and I was glad he had volunteered to conduct the service. He was also quite happy to hold it at the chapel, as his own church was far too small for the expected crowd.

I had never got religion. I had never seen God as having some omnipotent answer to my problems.

I was early. I had arrived at the chapel an hour ahead of time on purpose, because I had things to do and wanted to be sure everything was . . . right. Also I needed some time alone there, with her, one last time before anyone else arrived. Before I was obliged to become the courteous handshaking, grieving brother.

I looked about the chapel at the neat rows of chairs and the flower-filled urns placed attractively in niches in the walls. It looked very nice. Very formal and very expensive. The flowers were white lilies. With their fine, pale green leaves and long stems, they were elegant and feminine, I thought, and the florist and the funeral director had agreed. Perfect flowers for a young woman.

I had asked for no flowers to be sent by others, but instead for gifts to be made to the Cancer Council. Hardly connected to Maria's death, but it had caused our mother, Amelia's, death. So, there was a family connection.

At the front of the chapel was a small, low stage holding a polished timber lectern for the speakers to use. And in the center of the stage, on a stand, was Maria. Her coffin, waiting silently and patiently, holding what was left of her. Ready to be returned to the earth she had so recently been brought out of.

I walked up to the stage and stood beside her, looking at the dark, polished wooden casket with its genuine brass handles. I felt them to make sure she had what she had paid for, and they felt real to me. Solid. Reliable. Dignified.

Maria had waited patiently in the earth for so long to be found. And I wondered vaguely if in the end she was found because she had become tired of waiting. Thinking about it, I couldn't remember my sister ever being patient when she was alive. I best remembered her yelling at me and chasing me about the house as I laughed at nothing, or at her, for chasing me.

Now she was here inside this box.

"You're early,"

I jumped at the interruption, turning to find the undertaker standing behind me politely.

"Yes. I wanted to check on things. It's looking good," I replied, nodding vaguely at the chapel and the flower-filled urns.

"We'll have the floral arrangement for the casket here any minute now," he replied, and I remembered I had ordered another long spray of lilies to place on top of it.

"I have a photograph," I said hesitantly, "Of her, Maria," I added, handing him the plastic-wrapped package I had been carrying tightly under my arm. "I wondered if it could go on her casket, or nearby, so people are reminded what she looked like."

He unwrapped it. "So this is Maria?" he said quietly. I nodded. "A beautiful young woman," he said, in an understanding, but professional voice. "Very tragic," he added appropriately.

Then he sighed. A long, deep breath pulled in, then let go.

"You saw her, her remains, didn't you?" he asked.

I nodded, not wanting to dwell on that now.

"I'm sorry. But it means you understand that I had no idea what she would have looked like. I have never had anyone like her before, someone so young who was murdered and not found for so long," he said slowly, still gazing at the photograph. "Such a long time . . . and still no closure."

During the last four weeks I had looked for closure, expecting to find it any day. The discovery of Maria's body had, instead, exposed far too many things inside me that I had buried or altered in my mind over the intervening years.

"The photo?" I reminded him.

"Sorry. But I've got two daughters of my own—grown up now." He said it apologetically. "Yes, I think it would be very appropriate to have this sitting up on her casket. I will leave it here for now, and when the other wreath arrives, we can arrange the two together."

While he talked, he had rewrapped the photograph and set the parcel down carefully on the polished wood.

"Now I had better go and see to the other arrangements," he said, smiling quietly and slipping away.

I returned to gazing at Maria's casket. My parents had idolized her, even before she was gone. My mother had little interest in a son; I was my father's responsibility. Boys to her mind caused trouble and had it easy; it was girls who needed and deserved attention.

But I'd never been the son my father really wanted either. He'd wanted some big, confident soccer-playing boy who might one day grow up to be a real player. Maybe even play for Australia in the Soccer World Cup. I knew in hindsight that that had been his unspoken dream for me. But I'd been a disappointment in sports. I'd been a big disappointment to him in most ways, even before my sister disappeared. And then she was gone and I was all that was left for them.

In the beginning, both of my parents' lives had been totally centered on searching for Maria, on finding her. While they searched I had been left alone at home and had learned to cook my own dinner and get my own breakfast. Sometimes I'd had to take the money from my mother's purse to buy food, as my parents had other, far-more-important things to think of.

I felt an unexpected, but powerful, wave of anger and bitterness at what it had been like for me back then. I remembered the resentment I had felt toward Maria for going away and leaving me with all that to deal with. And my resentment of my parents for caring more for the dead than the living. Because after a short time, weeks only, that is what almost everyone had said, that Maria was dead.

But mine was a tired, worn-out anger that subsided quickly. And the bitterness had soured, then faded, with time.

Of course others, even some of those who to my parents' faces had said she was dead, had whispered that Maria had probably run off. A young woman escaping a strict father by running off with some boyfriend. So, at times I had also resented the girl who was away enjoying herself somewhere with another boy, or a man, while I was stuck there in the misery she had left behind.

Then one day, thirty-two years after she went missing, Maria had been found by some council workers who were digging up a damaged culvert outside Broken Hill. A truck had left the road and rolled, cracking it. And they found her under the concrete in a wooden box and the remains of her school uniform, so she had apparently been there in the dry, hard ground of the outback for over thirty years.

Suddenly it seemed unlikely she had deliberately run off, or if she had, she certainly hadn't enjoyed herself for long.

It had come as a shock to have Maria found so suddenly and finally like that. To have the unanswerable question that had shadowed my life finally answered. Maria was dead. She had always been dead.

Standing beside her coffin, I wondered vaguely if she had been annoyed at being disturbed in that other grave, or if she was glad that everyone now knew at least part of what had happened to her.

Because though the police seemed to know something, they didn't seem to be in any hurry to discover more. But there had been no doubt at the inquest that she had been murdered all those years ago—probably within hours of her disappearance because they knew she had been buried outside Broken Hill within two days. Apparently they had unexpectedly good information about when the culvert had been first built.

CHAPTER 2

Four weeks before the funeral I was oblivious to Maria's fate. And she had been a part of my life.

On Wednesday morning I had looked at myself in the bathroom mirror as I ran my fingers up my neck to my chin and on to my bottom lip. Smooth, I thought. Smooth as I liked it to be each morning when I'd shaved, smooth skin like a woman's.

But no more of that, I thought. Work. So no more. The time for that was the coming weekend. I shook my head to clear away the thoughts, but I still had a small wave of arousal from them. Then when I reached down and tugged at myself vaguely, I suddenly remembered what Allison, my ex wife, had said.

Near the end of our marriage she would stand there, fists clenched in anger, saying, "You like sex well enough James, just never with me. And if you lost your right hand, you'd be celibate."

Sometimes she would yell it so loudly that I wondered if the neighbors heard her. And I would be stupidly annoyed too, as Allison knew very well that in that, at least, I had always been ambidextrous.

Then Allison had met the German tourist, and in a few days she was gone. Before things got really nasty. I had often silently thanked the German for making my life so easy just then.

How Allison and I had ended up in the same bed together was a mystery to me.

"Bitch," I said to my reflection.

I looked in the bathroom mirror at my forty-two-year-old face. And for a moment I knew I wasn't middle-aged yet and would not be for years, because I didn't want to be. I couldn't imagine feeling middle-aged until . . . until at least . . . "Sixty," I said out loud. "Not until I'm sixty. That seems far enough away to deal with."

But I also knew quite well why I had married Allison. I had not wanted to be left alone when the music stopped in the game of musical chairs that was marriage and family. I had wanted the dream too. I had missed it for too long and I wanted it desperately. But in the end it hadn't worked; there had been no dream. Just confusion and guilt. Frustration and hurt.

I had tracked Allison down to Thailand, and she had signed the divorce papers and taken the money I had offered her, happy that she and the German could continue their Asian odyssey together, while I had been free, and alone again. But not entirely alone, and not entirely free.

In the mirror I saw my familiar, slightly foreign face, with its olive skin, dark eyes, and dark hair. Hair that was starting to turn gray. The gray was mainly at the temples, where it formed silver wings. But there were also obvious strands of silver above my forehead that gave me a mature and sophisticated look. Not an old look, I was sure. A masculine, mature look.

But I missed the darkness of it when I had been young. The darkness was important, I knew. And the coming weekend my hair would be dark again, and long.

I went to Sydney every month for my night away. My escape. My satisfaction. I went with Maria, I became Maria, and I was free.

I was going to Sydney the coming weekend. Even thinking of it aroused me. And the dull ache I had in my balls would grow until Saturday night when it could be fully released.

CHAPTER 3

What was now sitting wrapped up on top of Maria's casket was the framed photograph of her that had stood on top of our mother's television set until her final trip to hospital. She had taken it there with her and sat it on the cabinet beside her bed and died with it there.

Until the previous day, I hadn't looked at the photo since my mother's death. But I had decided I wanted something at the funeral to remind everyone, including me, of not only how Maria had looked but also to make her real, to remind them of who she had been.

When I found it and looked at the photo again, I had been shocked. In her photograph Maria now looked different to the way I'd remembered.

Maria. I'd had an image of her as a slut. That was how she had been explained in my mind and what she had been for me. And that was what I used to see in the photograph. And that was what I couldn't see there any more.

Now when I looked at her picture I saw a beautiful young woman, standing, foolish and uncertain, on the edge of life. On the edge of an adulthood she would never reach. And it had brought tears to my eyes.

Suddenly I was crying. In spite of the missing years, she was suddenly a violent, unexplained death in the family, and she was part of me.

I had wept for her loss, properly, for the first time in my life.

There was a school photo of myself taken a couple of years after she went that I kept sitting on a side table with other family photos. And when I had looked at the two of them together I had seen what I had obviously known back then. I had seen the uncanny similarity between us that had existed briefly when I was in that stage between boyhood and manhood. When I had been smooth skinned, fine featured, and dark haired. I had indeed looked very like her once. And that, I thought, began to explain a lot of things more clearly to my adult mind.

* * * *

My father had been the first to give up the searching because he'd had to go back to work. He'd been a builder, and he had argued that the building could only stop for so long before he lost his business. And later he had changed.

Something inside had twisted the memory of the daughter he had adored. Perhaps to punish her for leaving him.

My mother had always been at home, but for a long time she had continued to go out each morning, as soon as my father had left for work. Gone out looking for Maria. What she had expected to find I had no idea, nor where she had gone, or what she had done.

Mysteries. Now it was so far in the past I could wonder about it. At the time I had only wanted it all to go away.

Meanwhile in the empty house they'd left behind, I would get a chair so I could reach the breakfast cereal up in the high cupboard where it was kept, and I had learned to iron my school shirts. I was always fussy about my uniform, and it was in those first months, or weeks perhaps, that I had learned to iron neatly.

After the first weeks of shared desperation, my parents had become disconnected from each other, as they had already become disconnected from me. And, even as young as I was, I vaguely knew we had ceased to be a family and become no more than three people sharing the same house.

When my mother finally stopped going out to search for Maria, she had taken to spending her days in her daughter's room, crying endlessly while she fondled Maria's things and tried to reach out to find her spirit. That was what she said, that she sat in there trying to feel Maria's spirit. Searching for a message to tell her where her daughter was. But she never received one.

As far as I knew Broken Hill had never figured at all in my mother's thoughts either. So much for the psychic bond between mother and daughter, I thought sadly.

There had also been too much money in Maria's bankbook; the thought was still fleetingly there, even though I now knew where the money had come from. A young woman with too much money who people were saying had run off with a man. What sort of girl did that make her? We all knew. Well, I had thought I'd known.

We bring our preconceptions of people to how we look at things, how we see them. We see with our emotions, and that changes how things, even photos, look. I know it does for me anyway. Sometimes. Certainly it did with her.

The florist arrived with the long arrangement for the top of the coffin and Keith came back with her. Together they arranged it. Then Keith unwrapped the photo that had been sitting there waiting and set it between the last blossoms on the two longest stems. It looked right there.

"There," he said, standing back beside me to survey his efforts.

Fine, I nodded. Any words I might have said catching in my throat.

Looking closely at the photo, the florist said, "Beautiful girl; such a terrible waste." Then she turned and left.

The photo was a final reminder to me that what was left of my sister was indeed inside the polished-timbered, brass-handled casket, sitting there under the transiently fresh and beautiful lilies.

CHAPTER 4

The first thing my aunt Rose said when I'd told her Maria had been found was, "Your mother would have been relieved to know where she is at last."

Part of me wondered if she would have been, though, because in the end the search for a sign from her daughter had become my mother's whole life. She had spent everything, her time and money, going first to religion for answers, then going from one psychic to another.

Our father and Maria used to argue a lot, but I'd known he'd preferred her over me. I knew that the arguing that went on between them was part of that. He argued with her because he cared. He cared enough about her to demand more and to expect more for her; he didn't want her to waste her life.

My father and I had never argued. To me he was just polite. Especially after the incident of the soccer boots.

When my sister was gone, my father had made one last attempt to have the son he wanted. The soccer boots. He had spent a lot of money on them, and it had even been a big event to go and buy them.

We had gone into the city, just the two of us, and he'd taken me into the big sports store where all the real team's players got their uniforms from in those days. My father had told the assistant who served us that he wanted the same brand that Pele wore. The assistant had been condescending, making a point of letting my father know exactly how much they cost before he even went to get my size from the back room.

I knew my father had been insulted by the man's attitude, but there must have been nowhere else to go for those particular boots, because my father stayed and bore it, only letting himself go and swearing when we had left the shop with the precious boots sitting in their box inside a thick brown paper bag with string handles and the name of the shop printed on it.

The next Saturday he helped me tie them up when I wore them for the first game of the season. But I was quickly run over by a couple of bigger boys and had lain bruised and grazed on the grass, trying not to cry. I think it came home to him finally that day that I would never be the son he wanted me to be.

I don't even know what he did with them, I just never saw the boots again, and he never came to watch me play again. Which was a relief, because I could give up trying to play soccer and football after that. I'd never liked them, the roughness and the thumping, bumping pain and humiliation of them, and knowing I was never going to be any good.

A long time ago, I thought, pulling myself back to the present, to the chapel where the service would be held.

Soon it will be her funeral, I thought. I could bury what was left of her, but not the things that had flowed from her discovery, or those that had flowed from her disappearance. Her death. I could think of it as her death now, not just an inexplicable absence. But above all I wondered if I would live better knowing what had flowed out from her brief life and what I now knew about her death.

"No problems yet?" I asked Keith, the undertaker, as he came up to me again.

"No, nothing we haven't been able to handle politely. But it will be best if you give them something—a few words, a few photographs," he said calmly.

I'd come early, not only to make sure everything was in order, but also to avoid the media. The undertaker had arranged for some discreet security to keep the worst of the attention away. And I had been relieved to know I was safe from them for a while.

I wanted the media to go to hell, but knew he was probably right. "Whatever you think is best. Can you organize it?"

"I'll arrange a brief photo opportunity fifteen minutes before the service begins," he replied.

As the service was due to start in less than half an hour, I gathered he had already organized it and I felt annoyed at not having been told earlier. But I accepted the arrangement. Even I knew the media wouldn't go away empty-handed.

Maria's death was an unsolved murder, and her discovery had been a major local news item. Her original disappearance had filled the headlines of newspapers throughout the state over thirty years before, and a small town has long memories. It was accepted that she'd been murdered. There had been no dispute about that in the findings at the inquest, though they had described her death as being caused by a person or persons unknown. And that only added to her newsworthiness.

Surprisingly "murder" wasn't a word that I had ever heard my mother use in relation to Maria.

They seemed to know how Maria had died. But there was nothing broken that way—not the bones anyway. Obviously something had been broken, or stopped, or she wouldn't have been dead. But it had been something soft; her bones had had no story to tell. And they had lain there silently when I looked at them.

They say it's usually family. Family or friends; when someone is murdered. The murderer. Family or a friend; it's rarely someone the victim doesn't already know. When she was found I knew that there weren't that many people in our family back then. And I'd been sure she'd had no boyfriend, so the field was limited.

I wandered back to the coffin and, bending over a fraction, inspected Maria's photograph more closely. The more I looked at her the more I could see that she had also strongly resembled our mother, and our aunt Rose. Our father may have loved her best, but while I was very like him, I could see little of him in her.

"Oh, James," a voice interrupted me, startling me. "Oh dear. You've got her photo there."

I turned to find Rose standing beside me, frowning at Maria's photograph.

"Oh. I had forgotten how much she looked like Amelia, like your mother."

"More like you, I think," I said.

My mother had died four years before, and the only blood relations I knew of who remained from her side of the family were her sister, Rose, and Rose's two daughters. Rose and I had become surprisingly close since then, and once a fortnight we had lunch together.

"Where's Cicely?" I asked, glancing around and missing Rose's shadow.

"She's outside with Linda," Rose replied, still staring at Maria's photo.

"And Frank?"

There was no answer.

Rose; her husband, Frank; and their two daughters completed the maternal list of relations. Both girls were grown women now, in body, if not also in mind. But both were younger than Maria, younger than me as well and hardly likely to have killed her. The idea of a couple of preschoolers killing someone was very black humor, and I'd laughed when I had first had the thought weeks before.

Frank. Well, Frank was Frank. He worked on the railways, and he always had. And I knew he would continue to for the few years of working life that remained to him. We didn't get along, but he had always done the right thing by Rose and the girls. And with their youngest, Cicely, it hadn't been easy. They had both made sacrifices for Cicely, but I thought Frank most of all. So, though I didn't like him, I grudgingly admired his stolid loyalty to his family.

"Is Michael coming? Your father," Rose asked, finally looking away from the photo.

My father was still very much alive.

I shrugged. I doubted he was, but I didn't want to say it and sound angry, when there was still plenty of time for him to appear.

There was a long silence. "I don't think so," I finally said, unable to bear the silence any more.

"How can he do that? Not go to his own daughter's funeral. It's not right. Not at all," Rose said, shaking her head but not expecting any answer. "How are you holding up, James?" Rose asked sympathetically. "So many people outside already. Who are they all? I hope it doesn't bother you that they have all come. I mean, most of them will only be here because of the notoriety."

"I don't care," I said quickly. "No. I'm pleased that anyone remembers her, even if it is only because she was in all the papers. Having just you and me and a couple of others here would be depressing."

I knew that I would have hated that, as well as being depressed by knowing that in the end my sister had lived and died without leaving any mark behind. I felt guilty that even I barely remembered the real her.

CHAPTER 5

The next person I saw arrive at the chapel was my neighbor, Ted. He'd wandered in as if he was lost, wearing a loose-check shirt and jeans and gazing about vaguely through thick-lensed glasses.

"This where it is?" he asked. He always asked the obvious.

He had been the one who had inadvertently let me know the police thought Maria might have been found.

He had called me at work to say that policemen wearing hats had been to my house. That was the sign—that they wore the full formal uniform.

I arrived home and waited for them to come back. But there had been a major pileup on the nearby motorway and no one visited me, while the wail of sirens continued for most of the evening as the police and ambulances went back and forth. They came back in the morning when the emergency was over, with Ted in tow. I'd opened the door and wanted them to stay outside, but they had invited themselves in with serious faces and formal courtesy.

"It's about Maria isn't it?" I'd said angrily. "My sister. Why you have to keep coming back I have no idea. You've got everything you need to identify her if you ever find her. I can't tell you any more."

"I'm sorry, Mr. Morgan, what we have come to tell you is that the body of your sister has been found and formally identified."

"What do you mean?" I looked from one to the other of them, still angry, and ready to say something about being bothered by them unnecessarily. It took me a few moments to take in what they had said.

"You have actually found her?"

I sat down heavily, stunned. I hardly heard what else they told me. When they had gone, having to let themselves out, I was disoriented; I found that Ted was still there, hovering in the hallway.

"I never knew you had a sister," he blurted out, "You never said anything. You want me to stay?" he added, obviously half eager for some gossip, but nervous of dealing with any display of emotion.

"No. It's OK; just go. Thanks, Ted, I'll be OK."

"OK. I'll just go," he'd said, backing up to the door and letting himself out while I sat there in a state of mild shock.

It was a while before I had done what I had to do and pulled myself together enough to get off to work. It was the first time I had ever been late for work, and everyone looked at me oddly as I walked into my office at Regal Plastics. Then Dana rushed in and closed the door, "Oh, James, I am so sorry," she gushed, trying to hug me as I fended her off. The discovery of Maria's body had been on the morning news.

My father was the first one I had rung after the police left. My immediate thought had been to call my aunt, Rose, but I had stopped myself, feeling that our father had a right to hear the news first from me. It was his body that had created her, his seed that had been planted and grown—part of his right to immortality that had been lost forever with Maria's death.

And I had realized then, right at the start, that when it came to potential murderers, there were a lot more possibilities on my father's side of our family. Including him. And the connection to the town outside which she had been found was

25

strong. Broken Hill lay 1,200 kilometers to the west of us. But, in terms of family, it was as close as my father's late brother, Nick.

Nick had done well for himself, building a small trucking business up from nothing to the point where someone offered him too much to refuse. He'd had the sense to sell, and I'd heard he'd watched with a shaking head and much disappointment as it was renamed and disappeared, being absorbed into the new owner's national road freight network.

One of Nick's first regular delivery contracts had been for an engineering firm with depots in Newcastle, Sydney, and Broken Hill. It had been part of a regular run for years. Once, when my mother had been in hospital, I had been sent off with my uncle Evan to do the run from Newcastle to Broken Hill and back. Uncle Evan had always worked for Nick. He had been a quiet man and never married. I remembered we had hardly spoken during the whole trip, sleeping at night in swags on the ground under the truck, though we had spent one night sharing a room in a Broken Hill motel before starting the drive back. It was the first time I had ever been anywhere alone, and the first time I had stayed in a motel. It was not long before Maria went missing.

After I had fed my surprised dogs an unusual breakfast and they had settled down, I'd picked up the phone and dialed my father. Glad it only rang twice before it was answered.

"Yes," a voice barked at the other end.

"Hello, Dad. It's me, James," I replied.

"So, when are you coming to visit me? Ken died last week. Do you remember Ken? He was my best mate here. Poor bastard fell down on his way to lunch, just like that, right in the passage, dead before he hit the floor they reckon."

I had no recollection of my father ever mentioning a Ken before, but it was a regular game he played with the latest death at the home. Every man who died was his best mate once he was gone. I now assumed it was my father's way of reminding me that he was still alive, right now, but might not be for much longer.

"I'm sorry to hear that, Dad. So how's the food?"

"Lousy, like always. So, what you calling for?"

"Are you sitting down, Dad?"

"Sure. Why? I always sit to talk on the phone."

"Well, Dad, the police have just been here. They came to tell me that they have found Maria. They are . . ."

I heard the crash at the other end of the phone line as my father hung up on me.

I was disappointed and upset, but not shocked. His reaction had been half expected. My father had not only been the first to give up the search for my sister, his daughter; how he felt about those of us left had also soon changed and he'd given us up too.

He had always worked long hours, and when he returned to work after Maria's disappearance, that didn't change. But when he got home we would eat in near silence, where before there had always been talk at the dinner table. And when he looked at me it was in silence and with no expression, and I felt he was looking at me as if weighing up my value.

Then he made that last effort to find the soccer-playing son he wanted me to be. After that failed, it seemed nothing had changed and we ate in silence still. But he rarely looked at me and continued to change underneath. Finally, he took to looking at my mother as if he were now weighing up her value.

And his attitude to his daughter slowly changed. So that toward the end he became dismissive of any talk about Maria. Finally, he would do no more when she was mentioned than grunt and toss his head and say loudly, "Hah. Maria was no good. We are better without her." My mother would sit in stony silence, and I would retreat to my bedroom or some other out of the way place. Others would simply be embarrassed.

Three years to the day after Maria went missing there was a blazing row between my father and mother. A violent one. Him shouting and throwing things, knocking her to the ground. My mother screeching and beating at him. Crying, wailing. I retreated to my bedroom, closing the door and hiding behind it, shaking. Terrified he would come after me too.

Thumps and bangs and my mother's sobbing and occasional wails had continued well into the night. I finally got to sleep, and when I woke in the morning, it was to a new world.

27

My father had stripped everything out of Maria's room and dumped it into the garage. Her things were scattered about the house and garden, along the path from her old room to where its contents now lay.

A long time ago. A bitterly angry and frustrating time.

I knew my father had never been contacted about any of the visits my mother had received from the police about Maria. He had never been involved again from the moment he walked out of our house for the last time.

My father had been fortunate to be out of it.

My parents had finally separated acrimoniously not long after the incident of my father's stripping of Maria's room and the dumping of its contents in the garage.

It was hardly surprising. Something like that either brings a couple together and binds them forever or it tears them apart. My parents were torn apart, and I was left floundering in the ruins.

CHAPTER 6

"James, isn't it? My name's Jennifer, Jennifer Toomey now, but I was Rogers when I knew Maria. At St Cecilia's," the woman on the phone said in a pleasant easy voice. The way she said it made me wonder if she expected me to remember her for some reason. The name meant nothing to me. "I'm calling on behalf of the girls she was at school with."

She was something on the ex-students association of Maria's school and had somehow got my number at Regal Plastics. For the two nights after they published the details of Maria's discovery in the *Moorebank Times* I kept my home phone off the hook. The first night had been endless calls from friends, acquaintances, and well-meaning people I barely remembered or had never heard of. I wanted peace, and real friends and family knew my mobile number—and my work number, of course.

"We're all so sorry to hear about Maria. I mean I am sure you knew she must have been dead. I mean I did too. All of us, all of her school friends did. But it's not the same, is it, as knowing definitely? Closure. That's important, isn't it?" Jennifer had added nervously but sympathetically.

"Yes. That's the fashionable term now. But I don't really see that it closes things, do you?" I'd replied, annoyed that everyone wanted to simplify things, when for me they were complicated and I was just starting to realize how complicated. "We still don't know what happened to her. Who was responsible. I don't even know how Maria died," I snapped.

"I'm sorry, James," Jennifer had replied, and the image her voice brought to mind was of a kind woman resting a hand gently on my arm. "I didn't mean to sound flippant about what's happened."

I felt slightly guilty for being so blunt with her. "Were you a close friend of hers?" I asked, wanting to start over.

"Close? I'm not sure. It was a long time ago. We were only kids. But, yes, I was one of the "group." You know, the group of girls that hung out together at high school. She was a bright girl. But shy too. And not always happy. I think your father was very strict. She wasn't allowed out often."

"It's so sad, James. I mean I have said we knew she was gone, but we all hoped, all of her old school friends, when it happened, that she'd run off with some hunk. She was quiet, but a bit wild sometimes, and we all thought at first she might have. She could be loads of fun, you know, but really unhappy at home. Which made it seem possible. But you were only a child, so you probably didn't know her well."

"No. I don't think I knew her at all," I responded truthfully. "I was only ten when she disappeared."

I knew how my Dad and Maria had often shouted at each other but, in spite of the arguments, I had never thought of him as being strict with her. And with my mother it was quite the opposite. To my mind she had been the favorite and was indulged in every way.

"They interviewed us all when it happened. The police. Do they think they will find out who . . . who killed her?"

"No. No, they don't seem to know anything," I told her, knowing it sounded unsatisfactory. "They have hardly said anything, and I have only spoken to someone over the phone. But it was a long time ago and they got nowhere at the time so . . . . apparently it's not one of those old cases you hear about that they solve instantly because they have DNA or whatever."

"Oh, I'm sorry," she said. "We all hoped. Things have changed so much."

I grunted, unable to say anything intelligent. Knowing how I too had thought at first the police would have something from the past that would now make it all clear. Some magic clue.

"Call me if there's anything I can do. Or if you want to talk about Maria. I keep remembering things about her. It's surprising what my mind has kept at the back all these years that has now been stirred up and is coming out."

I suddenly felt a need to connect with this woman, Jennifer. Connect with someone, someone apart from Aunt Rose, who had known my sister when she was alive. Someone apart from family. I desperately wanted to talk to this apparently genuine, nice-sounding woman who had really known her—and known her as only someone Maria's own age could have.

"Can we meet?" I asked Jennifer impetuously. "Coffee this evening. Lunch. Something. I'd like to talk to someone who really knew her," I babbled in a nervous rush.

Jennifer hesitated a moment, "Yes, I suppose so. Yes, if you want to. This evening? I have an appointment in Wangi at 5:00 p.m. Would 6:00 be OK?"

"Fine, terrific," I said, glad it was going to be soon. "I live in Moorebank. Does that suit you?"

We agreed to meet at the Andalusia Café, and I hung up the telephone with my head spinning. Questions came and went. What had my sister been like? Had she had a boyfriend? Had she been . . . ? Had she liked . . . ? A million things. What might have happened? Who had she known?

I doubted that Jennifer really had any answers for me. But no one seemed to have any answers, even the police. They had also called me at work not long after Jennifer had. I think they had just been letting me know they hadn't completely forgotten the case.

It had happened before, once before I left home, and twice afterward. The police coming to the door and talking about the possibility that Maria had been found. Of course, the hopes were unfounded each time, and on each occasion it had been a painful, pointless, emotional minefield with my mother.

My first thought when the police had arrived this time was that if my mother was still alive this would be another one of those awful times when she would be on the phone to me at all hours of the day and night. Crying and going on endlessly about my sister, "Saint" Maria.

When Maria had first disappeared I had been too young, and too disinterested, to get involved in any adult way. It had washed over me like someone else's war in another country, glimpsed only through deprivations at home and other's suffering.

My parents crying in the night. Short tempers. All sorts of weirdoes coming to the door and being let in. My parents going out at odd times because there had been a call. Answering the phone whatever time of the day or night it rang. In case.

In case what?

I'd often wished she would leave before she did. But when it actually happened the drama of her disappearance had made my life far worse, not better.

As a child I'd imagined that if she'd gone deliberately she'd have enjoyed keeping it a secret. For some reason I'd thought she was a sly girl. I had no idea why.

Of course, typically my wife, Allison, had got in on the act the last time it happened. She and my mother had made my life a misery, dragging out absolutely nothing for months. Probably one of the reasons I was now happy to settle for the company of my dogs, I'd often thought.

But this time the two young policemen had been brief.

"There are no doubts, sir," they had said, as they stood in my study. "I am afraid that it is definitely her. The dental and DNA evidence proves it."

CHAPTER 7

When we met at the Andalusia Café I discovered that Jennifer Toomey was as genuine and bright in person as she had seemed earlier that morning on the telephone.

She was the one who had suggested the café overlooking the lake for our meeting, and she arrived dead on time, something I rarely seemed able to do.

"Hello, James," she said brightly, as she handed me a business card.

I looked down at it, surprised. It said Jennifer Toomey— Realtor.

"So you're in real estate?" I asked lamely.

"Yes," she replied, smiling and looking out across the lake for a moment.

It isn't often that a woman stirs something inside me, but Jennifer did. And I wondered if I had sensed that on the telephone. She had to be at least seven or eight years older than I was, but, with her blonde hair and fresh face and good figure, she could easily have passed for a lot younger.

She turned back to me and bubbled on. "What a fabulous day, I think I've made a sale too, which makes it even better. Do you know the big house in Tilbury Street?"

"The one that's for sale?" I replied idiotically, "I mean the ochre and yellow place overlooking the lake? The one with the lap pool and the mass of tinted glass?" I added, trying to sound slightly intelligent.

"Yes, that's it! Well, it was my listing, and I think the offer I just got will be acceptable to them. It's such a fabulous house I was afraid one of the other agents in the office might have gotten a buyer in first."

Then she looked me over appraisingly. As if I were some property she had to value, which she wasn't quite sure about, because it was a bit unconventional, "I'm sorry. I'm babbling on about work. And you have just found out you have lost your sister. I'd like to be able to sit here and enjoy the view without having to worry about the time, but I have to be somewhere else at seven. So, what can I tell you about Maria?"

I understood and got down to business. "What was she like? What did she think? What did she want to do with her life? I didn't know her at all," I replied, before pausing a moment. "And did she have a boyfriend? Was she seeing anyone? Also, I wondered if she ever said anything about anyone in the family causing her problems—a man? You know what I mean."

Jennifer laughed a clear, open laugh. "You don't want to know much do you?" She looked out at the lake again and sighed. "I'm sorry James, we were so young. We giggled a lot. We didn't talk seriously about life." She looked back at me. "Have they got some ideas about what happened?" she asked, frowning. "The police?"

"No, the police don't seem to be want to say much. Understandable, I suppose." I wasn't sure quite how much it would be appropriate for me to say. "You don't know anyone else in my family, do you? There is no direct evidence, but coincidences that make me curious, and I wouldn't want to say anything that might cause problems."

"As far as I know I don't know anyone else who would be involved. And I promise I won't mention any names, if I do talk about it." She stopped, frowning. "I don't want to have to promise not to talk about it, because I still see a couple of old school friends regularly. And I know I won't be able to stop myself from telling them about meeting you." After she said this she was serious again. "Those friends may even know something I don't that's useful for you."

I was glad she was so honest. As she said, a promise of total silence was likely to be worthless. "Her body was found in a wooden crate buried under a culvert on a road outside Broken Hill."

"Such a long way away! I read about her being found near Broken Hill in the paper, but it didn't say anything about her being in a box."

"Yes, and because it's so dry there, she was quite well preserved, I think." And apparently there were still bits of her school uniform on her. So she had died, soon after . . ." I hesitated. "Anyway, an uncle of mine used to have a freight contract to deliver machine parts for an engineering company out there. I made the trip on one of his trucks once when my mum was in hospital. And I remember he had long wooden crates in the back of the truck with machined steel shafts in them. And those crates were very like the one Maria was found buried in."

I paused, hearing what I was really saying. It sounded like an accusation. And in my mind, of course, it was.

"Unfortunately, my uncle's dead now, or perhaps it's fortunate for him. He also had a son a bit older than Maria who was a well-known troublemaker, good looking, very popular, but trouble. He was killed in a car accident about five years after Maria went missing."

I omitted to say that it had been a stolen car and that he was being chased by the police when it happened.

"They were a close family on my father's side, an old-fashioned stand by each other, regardless, sort of family."

I shrugged, wanting to disassociate myself from them and their narrow-mindedness and rejection.

"Oh, I see," Jennifer said slowly, obviously full of curiosity. "So, you think maybe someone in your family killed her, and then your uncle took the body and hid it where they hoped it would never be found?" She gazed out at the water glittering peacefully in the sunlight and gave a theatrical little shudder.

"How awful," she continued. "So, what did she say about men or boyfriends? Like I told you, she was quiet but could be a lot of fun too at times. The trouble is she wasn't serious, you know what I mean? She wasn't someone who would tell you all the details about something private. We knew she wasn't happy at home, but she didn't ever actually say it. It was just the impression she gave because she would clam up if people said nice things about their parents or about arranging to go somewhere as a family. And often when we arranged to go out as a group, to the movies or something, you knew she wanted to go, but she would just say nothing. Then she'd occasionally turn up, really happy to be there and lots of fun to have around, but obviously not able to plan for it. So, you knew it was because of the way things were at home."

What Jennifer said sounded odd. I had always thought of Maria as coming and going as she pleased. When my father shouted at her about going out, she would shout back and seemed to ignore him. It went no further than them briefly shouting at each other. I realized that I thought of her as rather spoilt. Both my parents' favorite.

"She never mentioned a boyfriend; she never went anywhere with anyone in particular?" I asked.

"No, never that I knew of. We hung out in a group of about eight or ten girls. Sometimes we'd meet up with a group of St Joseph's boys and a couple of the boys really liked her. She was very pretty and . . . and she flirted, yes, but in a quiet way. She never went out with any of them, I don't think, or encouraged anything serious. I went out with one of them a few times, and I asked her to join us—the boy I was seeing had a friend who was keen on her—but she never did. We did think there was someone she was seeing who she didn't want people to know about. I think that the impression I had, though, was that she was seeing someone her parents wanted her to see. Someone we would think was very uncool. I don't know why I thought that. It was rather imaginative of me. But now I wonder if maybe it was just that home was really strict and she couldn't go out." She stopped, gazing out at the lake for a few moments before turning back to me. "Was your father really strict with her?"

"I would have said the opposite," I replied honestly. "And you don't know who she may have been seeing?"

"No, sorry," she said, obviously thinking. "I am not sure why I even thought there was someone, and I didn't mention it to the police. I don't know what was going on with Maria. I'm sorry. You don't mind if I ask the other girls what they remember, do you? I still see Pat. She used to catch the same train home as Maria. I know she had to speak to the police a couple of times. They asked her all about their last trip home together from school on the day Maria disappeared. If she knew something she didn't think your sister wanted people to know about, like meeting a boy, then Pat's the sort who would have kept quiet about it forever. Even though that mightn't be sensible."

I couldn't see any reason why Jennifer couldn't talk to Pat. And we parted on the understanding that if she found out anything interesting she would call me.

Watching her walking off, my eyes followed the roll of her hips and part of me wondered how long it would be before I could call her. Because I thought it would be nice to see her again, and it was a while since a woman had made me feel like that. I was not really expecting her to ring me first.

I had always wondered if my father had been involved in Maria's death. Parents are so often involved in the death and disappearance of their children, rather like husbands usually being the ones who kill their wives.

And I realized then that all I really knew about the actual events at the time Maria disappeared was that one day she didn't come home from school. I definitely needed to know more about that day. And it was now time I finally did some research and asked Rose for more details.

CHAPTER 8

Before Maria disappeared I occasionally explored our rather cluttered garage out of curiosity. Then later it was the place I often went to escape the tension inside our house. And after my father had stripped Maria's room, it was there that I had found her clothes thrown untidily into the big old wardrobe at the back. Oddly, my mother never returned them to Maria's room and recreated her shrine. But her life itself had become a monument; she didn't really need a room any more.

Once my father had gone I had spent more and more time in the garage. In the house with my mother, I was overwhelmed by her bitterness, her resentment, and her frequent lectures on the evil of men.

Murder wasn't a word that I had ever heard my mother use in relation to Maria, but she had said plenty of things about men raping, torturing, and killing girls and young women. According to her, all men were obsessed with sex and would rape any girl, or woman, who didn't give it to them. They would rape their wives even, she'd hiss with bitterness.

Now as I waited for Maria's funeral to start I wondered if my father had forced my mother to have sex with him when things were falling apart. If he had hoped that satisfying that basic shared urge was a way to reconnect with her or had simply been so desperately in need of release from all that was going on he had taken it for himself.

Yes. In my mother's mind all men were evil once Maria was gone. After my father had left, it was worse, and the only one she had to vent her rage at was me. At thirteen I was classed as a man in her book and accused of all those things that "men" did. And all sex was definitely part of men's evil. Those parts of me that made me a man were the cause of evil, and becoming aroused I was told repeatedly was the worst evil.

Looking back now I can understand something of how both my parents must have felt. At least in the beginning. And even later on. My mother had never actually been able to accept that Maria was dead, even though she occasionally said she did.

I know myself that you never really give up hope. An airline lost a dog of mine once. Somehow it was let out of its crate and jumped off the airplane when it was stopped at a remote airport that serviced a large mining community.

Not the same thing to many people, perhaps, as losing a daughter or a sister. But for me it was close enough to make me understand how it would feel. I remember vividly what it was like for me just then. Remembered the awful uncertainty of not knowing what had happened to my pet. And I had also thought, "so this is how it feels." Suddenly feeling for my parents, and understanding them, as I hadn't been able to before. Understanding their helplessness and guilt.

I'd flown up there to the mining community and spent two days walking up and down narrow bush tracks calling out her name, "Polly, baby; here, Polly," but nothing had happened. She didn't come to me.

We had found Polly's paw prints in the dust mounded at the side of the tracks that ran through the surrounding bush. Small paw prints intermingled with the bigger ones of the local dingoes. But no sign of her. It had been perhaps seven years ago. But I still remembered it all vividly.

Then two weeks later someone had found Polly.

I had been wondering how much longer I should advertise. Wondering what was the time you allowed to pass before you tried to give the missing up and get back to normal. Wondering how I would bear it if it had been my child instead of my pet dog that was missing.

A couple of teenagers had spotted Polly and chased her in their car, following her up a track not far from the airport runway until she had stopped at a big puddle, she always hated water, and they had got out and caught her.

I received a phone call, and she came back as if nothing had happened. A couple of kilos lighter, a sore foot, scratches on her chest where she had moved through rough grass and the sharp debris that lies on the floor of the bush. Nothing else, suddenly the waiting and heartache was over.

But not really over, it took time to sink in that she was back. For the next couple of days I went to work and occasionally found myself thinking about what I should do, about looking further for her. Then I'd remember she was back at home, mentally pinching myself to be sure the relief was real, not imagined.

So now that I'm a grown man I can understand my parents' helplessness when their daughter vanished, their need to listen to every promise, to take everything seriously. To hope.

But I also know that there comes a time when you have to accept that you can never do enough trying to find what has been lost. Whatever you do, however hard you search, for however long. You can always feel guilty that you hadn't done enough. What's important is to recognize that the time comes when the chance of finding what you are looking for is so remote that it's foolish to continue doing everything.

One day it's time to get on with living.

I reached out and ran my hand along the side of Maria's coffin. It was solid and permanent. And I was alive. Much of the hold she had had on me was already gone, and once she was buried I knew that even more would fall away. The consequences of her life would remain to hold others more strongly, but I would be freer than I had ever been.

Unfortunately, my mother was never able to do that. To get on with living. My father had done it in his own way, by making another life and rejecting all of us.

40

CHAPTER 9

My aunt Rose had been a young woman with two small daughters when my sister went missing. And after I heard that Maria had been found I couldn't wait till the next Saturday when we had arranged to have our usual lunch.

I had lunch with my aunt Rose regularly. About once a fortnight. When I called her, it hadn't been much more than a week since we had last met. Just before I was told they had found Maria. Rose was surprised when I rang saying I wanted to see her as soon as possible. But when I said it was about Maria, she apologized, saying she had other things on her mind and that of course we could meet. I was surprised and also a bit hurt that she hadn't realized immediately that that was what I would want to talk to her about.

"Would tomorrow be all right?" she said.

It was a weekday and I didn't want to be rushed. "What about tomorrow evening?" I asked, "Dinner instead of lunch for a change. I don't want to have to hurry back to work."

Going to visit Rose at home would have been easier, but I rarely went to her house. Her husband, Frank, made it difficult. I had never felt welcome or comfortable. I thought of him as the frozen man. He worked nightshift and had done so since Cicely was a toddler. When the girls were young, Rose had worked part time and he had shared caring for them with her, knowing that Cicely would possibly never be able to be left alone.

When I visited, Frank always sat glued to his chair in the lounge room with the TV turned up unbearably loud. And if you weren't half deaf like him, it was impossible to stay in the same room. When I had made the effort to speak to him, Frank had rarely done more than grunt. I had given up and rather than try talking to Rose over the noise of the TV, I met her at a café.

I had heard people say Frank was easygoing and friendly. I had never seen it.

Rose wouldn't come to my house anymore. She had been to my new house twice. The first time she had come my dogs had frightened Cicely, who had opened the glass doors to the patio a bit and one of the dogs had squeezed in and immediately started jumping up on her. Cicely had started screaming mindlessly.

She hadn't been hurt, not even scratched, but Rose had rushed her away, back home. The next time they came Cicely had a panic attack at the front door and they had left immediately. Rose had told me angrily that I should get rid of my dogs, and they hadn't tried again.

I knew that those things all denied me an informal closeness with Rose that I would have liked to have.

Rose was surprised by the evening invitation, but as usual, whenever the opportunity arose, she was ready to go out and leave Frank to his TV.

We went to our usual café, Laska's, with its old-fashioned and well-worn dark wooden floor and furniture and its friendly staff who knew us. And even though it was evening, Rose had brought her younger daughter, Cicely, along, as she always did during the day.

Cicely smiled and dribbled a bit and had brought a book to read. She opened it up as soon as we were sitting down and then put on her glasses to read. I could see the book was upside down, as her books often were. But Cicely considered it as seriously as a judge reading the law.

"Well what's so important it couldn't wait a week? Not that I mind going out for dinner. It's years since I went out at night. And candles on the tables; how romantic. A bit hard to see the food by at my age, but I don't suppose they want to poison me anyway," Rose ended all of this with a laugh, obviously enjoying the novelty.

"I wanted to talk to you about Maria."

"Oh, what about her?" she asked with obvious surprise. "She's been dead for years, James. There is no point thinking about her. You need to move on. And what on earth do you want to know anyway?"

"What she was like. What her plans were. I mean, I didn't really know her. She was so much older than I was, and a girl," I said.

"Well, she was very pretty, and very confident and bright and full of herself. I think she was supposed to be going off to teachers college. Your father was always going on about her making something of herself," Rose said. Then, shaking her head slightly, she added, "She had so many things going for her."

I mumbled some sort of acknowledgement before saying, "And for some reason I had always thought she was . . ." I tried to think of what to say, how to put it, ". . . that she caused my parents problems with her behavior, before she disappeared." I paused, knowing that sounded meaningless, "That she was seeing boys a lot . . . and things," I added lamely and knew I had put it badly.

"Well, she was seventeen. I'm sure she wanted to go out with boys, but I can't remember any talk of one in particular, and your father would have wanted to know everything about him if there had been one. And she probably wanted to do things too, but back then girls were supposed to pretend they didn't." Rose laughed a deep throated laugh that surprised me.

"Your father was always a difficult man James. He seemed to think she should be a saint. And, unfortunately, she was the kind who answered him back as she got older," Rose added as she considered the menu, peering at it in the dim light. "I can't read a thing, James. Be a good boy and tell me what this says, will you?" She wiggled the menu at me in annoyance.

I dutifully read the menu out to her, having to peer myself without my glasses. I normally only needed them for small figure work, not menus. Another sign of getting older, I realized.

When we had ordered, I returned to my questions. "So, he would have called her names? I can remember there always seemed to be arguments at home before she went. I can remember wishing she would leave before she did, because it was often unpleasant."

Cecily suddenly laughed as if she had read something funny in her upside down book. Then she turned a couple of pages over slowly as Rose and I sat in silence and watched her.

"Like I said, she answered your father back," Rose finally said. "They were very alike, James—very likeable when they wanted to be, but stubborn. Very stubborn and argumentative. You're nothing like him in temperament, though you've got his looks. He was a very good-looking man when he was young. But you're not like your mother, either. I don't know who you are really like."

Rose paused, looking at me, as if she might have some inspiration.

I was pleased in a way that she didn't think I had either of my parents' temperaments; because I didn't want to be like either of them. "So, she wasn't a bad girl, Maria. I mean she wasn't a slut or anything?"

Rose laughed, and Cecily joined in, not wanting to be left out. Looking up from her book.

"Well, she was seventeen and still at school, I mean she might have been seeing boys behind the shelter sheds every lunchtime, but how do I know?" Roses sounded irritated. "I never heard him call Maria one, but according to your father, any girl out in public after dark was a slut. He went on and on about it when I started working evening's at the cinema. 'You're a brazen slut, Rose. I've seen you talking to the boys, standing out on the steps of the cinema in the middle of the night.' Rant, rant, rant." Rose leaned toward me across the table. "Your mother wasn't allowed out alone in the dark in case some man went after her. She got an afternoon job at the cinema too for a while, and when daylight saving stopped, she had to give up work. They had so many rows about her travelling home in the dark."

All this came as a revelation to me.

"So, he called you a brazen slut?" I said, and laughed.

Rose looked slightly annoyed.

"I'll have you know I was very popular when I was young," she said. "Frank could have had any girl he wanted, but he didn't look anywhere once we started going out together."

"Frank?" I said in surprise.

"Yes. He was very good looking, James." She smiled. "And he had a real way with him when he was young, but things haven't always been easy for us."

Rose glanced over at Cicely, and I knew that they hadn't had it easy with her. Originally, Frank started working nights so that Rose could work part time in the day, and he would be home to look after Cicely while she was gone. Now Rose didn't work, but he had stayed with working nights.

"He was offered a promotion to Sydney just after Cicely was diagnosed. He had to say no, of course."

"What happens to Cicely when you are both too old?" I asked.

"Linda will look after her, of course," Rose said confidently, as if there was no other answer.

Suddenly I realized that life hadn't been easy for Cicely's older sister, Linda, either. As far as I knew, she met her husband, Rick, in high school when they were both fifteen and hadn't ever had sex with another man. They had a small business that kept them going six days a week, and she had been responsible all her life, with caring for her sister to look forward to in her old age.

"How does she feel about that?" I asked.

"Linda knows what is right, James," Rose replied sharply, arching her eyebrows and looking austere. "And I am sure she will be able to call on you for help if she needs it."

I nearly choked on my food, but I wouldn't have dared argue with Rose while she was looking that way. I was suddenly seeing a side of her I hadn't seen before.

Finding out that my father had called Rose a slut amused me, but if he had got that so wrong, then what about Maria?

Had there ever been any boys or behavior for him to argue with Maria about at all?

"I must have heard my father calling her that when they were having their rows then, and being a child I accepted it was true and remembered it."

"That's not a nice thing to think about your sister, James." She frowned, then softened it. "But you didn't have a good childhood, I always felt sorry for you. Once I visited and you cooked me dinner while we waited for your parents to come home. Do you remember that? You were about twelve, and you made me sausages and instant mashed potato. I hate that Deb stuff, but I couldn't tell you that."

"I don't remember that," I replied, genuinely disappointed that I didn't remember cooking for Rose.

It was a memory I would have liked to have, me and her sitting down together, alone, to a meal I'd cooked.

CHAPTER 10

I was thirteen when my father left, leaving me alone with my mother. And at thirteen I was a child in a body that was rapidly becoming a man's.

I had never been an outgoing child, and after Maria disappeared I became extremely introverted, escaping mentally from my mother into books and fantasy. And often I escaped physically into the garage, where I found the other Maria, which I now realized was the most enduring fantasy.

At thirteen I was no longer a child, and when I opened the wardrobe door and looked in the mirror, I started to see her. Now that I had looked at my mother's favorite photo of Maria and my own photo at that age and seen the resemblance I knew why I saw her there when I looked at myself in the mirror. I really had looked very like her for a while.

Back then for some reason I had thought that she had done things with boys. And of course Maria had not been capable of any of the wicked behavior my mother ranted at me that men were capable of. Maria had been perfect, and sex had been part of her. She was made for it.

I can still remember digging about in the wardrobe and feeling her soft red jumper when I found it. I was immediately aware of the sensual feel of the fluff. I also remembered her alive, her breasts filling it, changing their shape. And I was aroused.

Aroused as I was usually afraid to be, knowing how wrong thinking of my sister like that was. Of how wrong and evil those urges I was getting could be. Of how it was those urges men had that had taken Maria away from us.

Then I had found and pulled out the small white vinyl miniskirt she had worn and I had held it up to my hips.

I turned and twisted it and then put it on and dropped my pants and rubbed my cock up under the skirt, and I came. I was looking in the mirror and I was Maria now, I was playing with myself, but I was a girl. I was her, and I was free to think of sex, satisfying my confusing needs hurt no one.

And since she was found, I had remembered. Remembered the white skirt and what I had seen.

I had seen her sneaking into the house through the back door one afternoon while wearing it.

Now that I knew she was dead I had recalled the memory of that memory. The morning the police had come and I was told she was dead I had looked at the white vinyl skirt lying on my bed, waiting to put it away. And in my mind I'd seen her hand holding a pink-striped wash cloth and stroking the front of the skirt gently, cleaning it.

It had all come back.

She hadn't noticed me, but I had noticed her, and I'd known that something was going on by what she'd done. She had come in quietly and headed straight for the bathroom. And I had followed behind. Curious.

And now I remembered too that she was always home before my father, but usually not much before. She arrived home from school long after me, and I knew it took her longer to get home on the train, but not that much longer.

Inside the bathroom she had wet the striped wash cloth and stroked it down the front of her skirt, smiling as she did so, smiling to herself.

There are things you know instinctively. Even at ten.

When she spotted me, she had smiled a knowing smile of adult power. "Go away little boy," she'd said quietly and closed the door.

So. I'd thought. As I'd packed the white vinyl skirt away, there had been a boyfriend. And deep down somewhere, I knew I had always known.

After the first time I had put on her skirt I often used to go and sit out there, in the back of the garage. Going through her things. I'd do it when I needed to, or just to escape because I couldn't stand being inside the house with my mother any longer. I selected what I fancied and put it on, always with the white vinyl skirt on, though. Then I paraded in front of the wardrobe mirror, seeing her there in the glass. I'd run my hand over my chest as I must have seen her do at some time, and I'd be masturbating, coming guiltlessly over or under the white vinyl skirt, as I knew other men had. I knew that. And it had been OK when she wore that skirt.

I looked at the spray of fresh innocent-looking lilies on top of the coffin and remembered feeling lost after I had been told about her being found.

"Well kids, it's wonderful to have a caring and supportive father, isn't it?" I had said out loud to my dogs in the evening, as I remembered my father hanging up on me.

I was talking to May, who was sitting next to me on the sofa, and the other four dogs resting by my feet on the pale-blue machine-washable mat. I wished I had a human to talk too, or more intensely, I wished I had a warm welcoming body to wrap my body around and enter. To lose myself in, to help me forget. And I had sat there in the increasing darkness of the evening, lost in the past, dragged back frequently by phone calls from acquaintances and friends—and the newspapers. Still trying to come to terms with what the police had told me.

Later in my bedroom I had remembered Maria in her white skirt, the memory coming as I neatly put away the clothes that I had left spread out on the bed, hoping to relive some of the weekend's sex.

There was now something improper about the little white skirt and tops. They looked dirty and sad. They made me feel uncomfortable.

The pleasure and the promise of freedom had suddenly gone from them, and for a moment I had been afraid of what that would mean. The white vinyl skirt, the latest of several, had stared back at me like some irrefutable and damning evidence of an unsatisfactory life.

CHAPTER 11

I'd had to see Maria. It had been too long. I remembered almost nothing about her, just a few images; one of her in that red fluffy sweater that was tight and showed her breasts. It was the first time I had noticed them. My young boy's mind had suddenly been caught by them. And I'd been unable to look away from the swelling mounds of her femaleness—until she hit me with a shoe she had been holding.

My lawyer spoke to the police and the morgue and was able to arrange it, and I think I was very lucky he had been able to. Though, when I had first seen her, that hadn't been exactly how I'd felt.

I had gone down on the train to see her, and I remember the ride vividly. Everything I had done during that day seemed to be part of a heightened awareness for me, and the train ride itself had been full of strange signs and images.

Not long after the train left Moorebank station it clunked along past a big orange and white cat that was sitting at the edge of the strip of rough ground running along the side of the railway line. Sitting erect and still, with its tail wrapped around its bum like an old china figurine, staring through the fence at the

51

fifth tee of the golf course. A couple of oblivious golfers preparing to hit off were caught in its gaze.

It reminded me that we'd had a cat just like that once. A ginger and gold striped animal with a mind of her own. And I remembered one afternoon Maria and I had been sitting watching television, her with the cat in her lap, while we both ate ice cream. The cat had jumped off her unexpectedly; the way cats suddenly do, knocking the bowl of ice cream from Maria's hand and onto the floor.

Of course it had fallen upside down on the carpet, dumping soft Neapolitan ice cream out. I clearly saw Maria trying to scrape it up, back into the bowl, and it was so soft that her efforts had just spread it about more and rubbed it into the carpet. I remembered laughing at her misfortune, the way kids do. Then our mother came in and saw the mess, and Maria blamed me for it and my mother believed her. Yes, in her book all boys were trouble.

It had been raining for most of the preceding three weeks and I wondered idly where the cat sitting beside the golf course slept. It had looked clean and plump, but there were no houses nearby. But it's the way with cats that they will roam wherever the fancy takes them, returning home or to another convenient house when they choose to, probably because they are ready to eat or be stroked.

In a moment it had been gone from sight as the train rattled on and I'd watched the bush pass by. The Gymea lilies were out and I could spot their big flamingo pink heads among the gums, a stem as thick as a man's arm sprouting up from clumps of green swordlike leaves. They grew in the bush outside the chain mesh fence that marched along each side of the railway line.

I was never sure just who the fence that had been put up along each side of the railway lines was there to protect. In many places there was nothing beyond it but undisturbed native bush, and in many other places it was damaged and wouldn't have stopped anyone from walking through it.

Finally, I had fallen into a reverie thinking about accounting, about how my work gave me answers without any personal involvement. It was a tidy thing to do usually; other people do the dicey, creative stuff. Not me. What I do is always straightforward, simple, clean. Understandable. I had discovered I liked that sort of simple certainty in my life.

Regal Plastics was nothing if not clean and honest. The old man saw to that. The place still bore his imprint and hadn't moved into the shadier modern world of financial expediency. Though how long that could last I had no idea. We still made money, but only just. Hardly enough to justify the investment in buildings and equipment. The business had long passed the point where the old man's family would have been financially better off moving the manufacturing off shore or selling up and investing the proceeds elsewhere.

It was the cloud that loomed on my horizon—the elephant in the corner, as the Americans say. How long would Regal Plastics continue to provide me with a well-paid job that was also simple and straightforward?

Part of me, I knew, needed a change, but the rest liked things as they were.

CHAPTER 12

The weekend before I was told they had found Maria I had done the drive to Sydney in warm sun and with my anticipation building as each mile passed. The Woolloomooloo hotel was modern and new and I had not stayed there before. I liked variety. And the woman was new too. I liked variety.

But some things never changed. When I was ready, I looked in the mirror and saw the long, dark hair and the white vinyl skirt, and that was enough. I saw what I needed to see to be set free. And my hand slipped under the skirt, and I touched myself guiltlessly.

When the woman arrived, I wanted to possess her completely, urgently. Mindlessly.

My own pent-up need would see me through the first part of the night. As soon as she was in the door, I had her pressed back against the wall, my mouth gulping at hers, my hand digging under her top and her bra, as I filled my palms with her breasts, squeezing them, pushing away the clothing.

"Hey, slow down," she gasped in a husky voice, pushing me back and pulling her mouth away from mine. But she softened the knock back by kissing me as she pulled away. "I have to go to the bathroom. You know. I have to get ready for you, baby," she said.

I stood back, reluctantly letting her go.

I ached, I needed, wanted her now. But this was an old familiar step in the night's action. And I sat on the end of the bed and waited for her to come out.

When we were done the first time, I lay back, knowing there was no rush to satisfy myself again. Now it was Maria's turn with the man woman, and I tossed back the long hair and bent to suck on her maleness.

It was an old game. It was a strange game. But it worked for me.

It had worked for me.

But now there was no one for me to hide behind. Maria was dead. It only took me a couple for days to realize that she was not only dead but gone in strange and unusual ways, and it had frightened me.

CHAPTER 13

As well as telling me she expected me to be ready to help Linda look after Cicely when the time came, Rose had dropped another surprise on me at dinner.

"I told Maria to go off and see the world when she got that money, you know. She would have had a wonderful time and still be alive, if she'd taken my advice. But she wanted to wait until she had it all before she decided what to do."

I had no idea what Rose was talking about, and mentioning Maria receiving money wasn't something I could let pass. But she was talking again, before I got a chance to say anything.

"And your father. Well. He was obsessed with her going to teacher's college. Told everyone she wasn't going anywhere until she'd qualified," Rose added before pausing to take a drink of wine. We never had wine at lunchtimes.

"What money?"

"Grandma Flynn's, dear. My girls and Maria were the only great-granddaughters. She was a great supporter of the emancipation of women was our Nana Flynn. She gave Maria some money before she died. She was about 100 when she finally decided she didn't have long to go, and the rest was to be split between Maria and my girls when she died. She only lasted a few weeks after Maria disappeared."

Rose paused, stopping to give the waitress the dessert orders for herself and Cicely. I was completely confused and in no mood to think of dessert. My head spun around trying to take in what Rose was saying.

"How much money?" I asked, stunned. "No one ever told me about her being given money."

"Well, I suppose they thought you might be upset, James. Getting left out completely, while she inherited. It was quite a bit, especially for then. The old girl had a big house at Double Bay, overlooking the water, which was sold when she went into the nursing home. I don't think they will ever find out who killed her."

"Who?" I asked, still with no idea what Rose was talking about, but suspicious that I should know. "Killed who? Why would anyone kill a 100-year-old woman?" I wondered aloud.

"What? Oh, who killed your sister. Are you feeling all right, James? You're not very bright today, are you? And you're looking pale. There is no point worrying about things. Is it work? I heard someone say they may be moving the Regal Plastics factory. They have closed everything else."

I was feeling a bit sick, actually, and sat back, not really hearing what else Rose was saying. I apologized to her and went to the men's room and locked myself into one of the cubicles for a few minutes of privacy. So, Maria had been given the money. But no one had told me in case I'd got upset. So here I'd been for these last four years sure she'd got it in some immoral way. And at her age. What had I imagined she had been doing?

Thinking about it now, the ideas I'd had seemed so ludicrous I couldn't believe I had ever seriously considered them. "Immoral" sounded like something that didn't exist anymore anyway. Everything seemed to be all right nowadays. I suddenly felt very stuffy and old-fashioned for feeling its meaning with such clarity. That I was an old-fashioned old fuddy duddy everyone kept telling me, and feeling that I had been acting like one was annoying.

One thing that had never fitted with the idea of Maria still being alive was that the money was still there when my mother died. I had found Maria's bankbook among her things, and the amount of money in it had shocked me—especially as my mother had often been short of money herself. When I discovered it, I knew deep down that if Maria had gone from choice, she would never have left her bankbook or the money behind.

Sitting in the toilet cubicle, I felt like laughing, as I realized that this really old-fashioned person was feeling stupid for having imaginative and apparently ridiculous suppositions about his dead sister. Yet, in the regular fantasy I indulged myself in Sydney, I sort of imagined I took over her body for sex. God, it was all too much.

CHAPTER 14

I wandered away from Maria's coffin after asking Rose to check that the supper would be being set out in the adjoining supper room as arranged. My wandering took me to the chapel's main glass doors.

Outside I saw that arriving cars were already filling up the first car park and several middle-aged women, who might have been from Maria's old school, were standing between two of the cars, chatting. Meanwhile, a middle-aged couple, who may have had nothing to do with my sister's funeral, were wandering across the lawn and looking down at the memorial plaques set into the grass in that section.

As I stood there aimlessly watching what was going on outside, an SUV with the name and emblem of the local TV station on its side pulled into the parking area reserved for the undertaker.

Time for me to perform.

I had become experienced at talking to reporters and cameras in the first few days after Maria's discovery was announced.

After I was told Maria had been found, a dozen emotions had moved through me daily, and my mind had kept on returning to Rocky.

My family used to visit Uncle Nick and his family regularly before my father left us. And Rocky. Well, he had been the flame that everyone revolved around. He was the smiling god. The one his three sisters and his parents had worshipped. Confident, good at everything, handsome. Adored by my father. And I had no doubt Maria had been drawn to him too. He had been irresistible to me, I knew. I had worshipped him, hung on his every word, and desperately wanted to be like him.

Rocky had been two or three years older than Maria, had his own car as soon as he was old enough to drive, and to my child's mind had been immensely rich. He always bought treats to give us when we visited, and I could remember Maria giggling once when he had demanded a kiss from her in return.

It had taken many years for me to realize what Rocky had really been. His family never seemed to see it.

My mother had cut all of my father's relatives off once he left. I'm not sure what she did, but we were no longer invited to visit anyone on his side of the family. And she had spilled the history of Rocky over me, as she poured her anger at men in general over me.

The stories she told about Rocky had sounded unbelievable at the time, and oddly that had been good. The fact that I couldn't believe what she said about Rocky had also sheltered me in a small way from the things she had said about men in general at those times. What I was sure were lies about my idol Rocky had angered me and helped me think the rest might be lies too and try to block it out.

But as I grew up and discovered more about people and the world, I occasionally thought of Rocky and her stories about him. And I had come to realize that whether or not Rocky was like that, there really were young men like him and that there may have been some truth in the tales.

Meanwhile, I also came to realize that the other things my mother had harangued me with were true of few men. There was no innate evil in a man's sometimes burningly intense need for sex. And any evil there might occasionally be had little to do with me satisfying my needs.

Later when I returned from Darwin and reconnected with my father's relatives, I had read between the lines enough to discover that a lot of what my mother had said about Rocky was probably true. Rocky had stolen cars and raped girls, my mother had said. And I wondered if at the time she had felt he was in some way responsible for Maria's disappearance. Now that there was a known Broken Hill connection my thoughts kept coming back to everyone on my father's side.

The main thing in Rocky's favor was that he'd lived in Sydney and had his choice of girls there. He hadn't needed the long, dangerous, over-two-hour drive up the old Pacific Highway that a meeting with Maria would have required. I didn't see Rocky as a man who'd waste unnecessary energy to get his rocks off. But who knows what another man will do?

I needed to talk to someone about that family, and the only one left I could talk to easily now was Dessi. Her father, Nick, had died of a heart attack ten years before, and Uncle Evan had gone a year before that. Dessi's two sisters were living 5,000 kilometers away in Perth, and I hadn't spoken to either of them for twenty years.

Thinking about it, I realized that it was also a long time since I had spoken to Dessi. Probably nearly a year.

I had meant to ask Rose what she knew about Rocky. It was one of the things I had planned to talk about when we'd had dinner, but the money business had taken my mind off the other things on my list.

Dessi lived on Sydney's northern beaches. I called her to arrange to visit, and she was cool. She had a part-time job. The only day that suited her was Wednesday. I wondered why she was working; she certainly didn't need the money. And on Saturday when I rang her the coming Wednesday had seemed a long way off. But I didn't think that it would be a good idea to try to change it or question her about anything just then. For some reason she seemed to be far from the friendly woman I remembered and instead I arranged to take the day off work.

CHAPTER 15

I returned to stand by Maria's coffin in the chapel to wait to be summoned by the press, and my thoughts turned back to the train trip I had taken to Sydney and what it had been like when I saw Maria there.

The Sydney morgue had seemed to be an intimidating place when I arrived at the entrance. Being passed by a middle-aged Southeast Asian couple who came staggering out clutching at each other in obvious grief had definitely made me hesitate about going in. I was momentarily uncertain about what I was doing there. But I also knew it had been too long, and that there had been too much fantasy.

Beneath the white sheet Maria had been even less than the Egyptian mummy remains I had prepared myself for. She was a badly moth-eaten unwrapped mummy, nothing more than small, black, desiccated remnants of skin and flesh on a dirty skeleton. The bones I could see were blotchy brown and yellow, with small tufts of wiry, rusty hair still loosely attached in a couple of the places where a young woman's hair grows thickly.

They were on her head, and even there, I saw with a shock, caught between her hips. I was fascinated for a moment by the way hair that was so glossy and rich in life had now become a few brittle threads, frozen to the bones.

She was rigid, twisted a bit, and a few bones had parted from the whole, including one foot, which was completely separated. I vaguely wondered why. But everything was neatly and recognizably laid out on the plastic sheet. A few small pieces of stuff, too large to be grains of dust, which had obviously fallen off her, lay on the sheet beside her. And the skeleton looked tiny.

I looked up at the spotty-faced young man who had escorted me in and who now stood opposite me on the other side of the trolley. "But, this isn't her; she was tall," I said in confusion.

I looked back in denial at what looked like some movie special effects creation and was supposed to be what was left of Maria. The woman I at times felt I became, the girl whose disappearance had ruined my life.

The bundle of dehumanized remains that was lying there was nothing.

But I had come looking for the cause of . . . of everything.

Maria had been a real person, a tall, vibrant, alive, young woman. What was set out before me was the shell of no one I remembered.

"About five foot three, 160 cm," the young man replied, shrugging. "Average for her age, she'd have grown a bit taller."

I had always thought of Maria as tall, never thinking that I had last stood next to her when I myself was only ten years old. It was, I realized later, the most shocking thing I ever found out about her—that she was so small.

So, I looked down at the moth-eaten, dried remnant of a small, unknown woman. Not Maria. I could not make that connection.

I did not see my sister in what I saw that day on the plastic-covered stainless steel trolley. I did not accept it was her until I looked at her photograph the night before the funeral. Then, finally, for some reason, I was able to reconcile those remains with being what was left of her.

The violent death of a small, young woman, whatever she was like, was somehow much worse than the violent death of a big, tall one.

But she had been a brazen slut! Brazen now no longer seemed right either, now that she had become small. Brazen wasn't for small girls.

And I had cried for her. Weeping for a small, beautiful, seventeen-year-old woman who had been foolishly and dangerously grasping at life. And who had died for it.

"I'm sorry," I'd gasped in the morgue, apologizing to the spotty young man. Just wanting to leave. "I'm sorry to have taken up your time."

I repeated it idiotically until I had left the room.

I was embarrassed by my reaction and confused by what I was feeling. I wanted to be out of there. There were no tears. I felt empty. Distant. I was embarrassed at having looked at a stranger who had been revealed so completely.

The morgue doors banged shut automatically behind me as if glad I was gone, another unwelcome visitor taking my equally unwelcome confusion away with me. I almost ran from the building, relieved at finding myself back on the street in fresh air and sunshine and in the everyday world.

Now I stood beside her coffin imagining those same remains lying inside it, no longer naked. I had bought Maria a dress to wear. To cover her. The sort of dress a girl wears to a high school formal. It seemed pointless, but it had also seemed right.

We had gone together to choose it—Allison; Rose; Cicely, of course; and me. And Allison had helped me pick it out. Rose had shaken her head, and I was sure she had only just held herself back from saying it was a waste of good money. But it had been Maria's money anyway. The whole funeral was being paid for by her, with what Grandma Flynn had left her all those years ago and had been sitting in her bankbook ever since.

Even knowing now how she had come by that money there was too much emotional baggage associated with it for me to want any of it to be left at the end. And if anything was left, it would be shared with my father. And I didn't want that either. He deserved nothing from her.

The parts had all come together for me in the recent weeks, and standing there, I felt tears on my face again and brushed them away. The casket reminded me of how fragile life is, how transient. How living every moment of life to one's best ability is all that matters.

CHAPTER 16

So far no one at all from my father's side of the family had arrived for the funeral, but there was still time. I didn't expect anyone, though, especially not Dessi, who I would probably not see again till my father's funeral.

Going south on the freeway to visit her had started out well but, as usual, seemed to mean getting into bad traffic as soon as I got near the Berowra turnoff. Once I had turned off toward Palm Beach it was stop, start, and slow all the way. It was long past time they did something about that road, I thought for at least the hundredth time. But all of my thoughts were negative and anxious that day.

I was not looking forward to my coming meeting with Dessi. So I was already expecting the worst when I finally arrived, and I wasn't disappointed.

Dessi and Ray's house is a big two-storey one, built of pale brick and of obviously solid, but slightly unfashionable, late 1970s design. I was sure that Uncle Nick had helped them to pay for it, as they had moved in as soon as they were married.

It sits a block back from the ocean, but the flatness of the area means that it has no view of the sea at all. And, just as I remembered, it was kept so immaculately tidy and clean that it still looked new. I doubted if there was even a dead leaf that had dared to land in the gutters.

Standing inside the wrought-iron gate and seeing how tall the pencil pines were, I realized that I hadn't actually visited the house since Allison left me. The pines stood in two rows, one running down each side of the garden. They now pointed at the sky from the air above the house, but when I had gone with Allison to Con's sixteenth birthday party, they had not yet reached the eaves. Too long ago. Over ten years, I realized guiltily.

I also saw that since my last visit a large concrete fountain had been installed in the middle of the front garden. It gleamed immaculately white, but was dry, a victim of the water restrictions that the drought had brought to Sydney.

Dessi's mother, Julie, had been the only one on that side of the family who had always kept in touch with me in my childhood. Every year she had sent me a birthday card and a small check. Until she died. I had rung up when her card didn't arrive to discover she was dead. Gone a month before. Until then I had not realized how completely cut off from my father's family I had become.

When I had returned from Darwin, there had been a period of years when I had been welcomed back into the family. Though by then it was only Uncle Nick and his wife, Julie; Uncle Evan; and Dessi's family, her two sisters having moved to Perth some years before. Alison had been welcomed too when I got married.

Dessi was definitely cool when she answered the door and let me in. "Hello, James. Come in. We haven't seen you for ages. You're looking well," she said politely.

It wasn't the gushing welcome I remembered. And there was no easy kiss or hug.

"You are looking well too," I replied, trying to sound bright. "How are Ray and the kids?"

"They're not kids anymore, James," she corrected me sharply. "Anoushka's having a wonderful time working in London. Did you know?"

I saw she was going to rub in our lack of contact. And I knew I partly deserved it.

"She got an exchange through her accounting firm. And Con has finished his masters. He's working with a big firm of engineering consultants in Perth. There are great opportunities there with the mining industry going so well over there, and he sees my sisters often," she informed me proudly, but also coldly.

I was wondering why her children had both left home so early to go and work elsewhere. There were plenty of opportunities in Sydney and closer to home. They had always seemed such a close family that I found it odd.

"And what have you been doing, James?" Dessi added.

It was asked as if she knew I had done nothing of any interest to her. She obviously didn't want me there.

Her attitude was a surprise to me. She had always had an easy, friendly manner when I had visited in the past. Like her mother's house, Dessi's home had always been ready to welcome visitors.

"Have I come at an inconvenient time?" I asked, trying to ease the atmosphere.

"No, James." She paused, regarding me with a grim, thin-lipped expression. "It's about Maria though, isn't it? Why you've come? She's been in all the papers. You don't call for years, and then suddenly here you are. I saw she was found at Broken Hill."

Dessi wasn't just sounding quite aggressive, her face was stretched and flushed. And her voice rose as she started to speak again.

"My father was a saint. A saint, James. And Rocky was a saint too. A wonderful brother. Wonderful. Who never hurt anyone. But when he was alive people were always trying to get him into trouble. You know why? Because they were jealous of him. He was so intelligent. So good-looking. He was a beautiful young man. But people had to try to pull him down all the time. It was sickening. Now the police call, asking where Rocky is, I say he died, and you turn up after not even bothering to call for years. Now you come, all trying to make some kind of innuendo against those wonderful men."

She stopped, either because she had run out of steam or was afraid of what she might say next. We both still stood in the middle of the wide hallway in the spotless, almost silent house.

Somewhere a radio or TV was on, but the sound was deadened and faint there in the cool hall. I hadn't even been shown in and offered a chair, or a cup of coffee, in a house that had always prided itself on its hospitality.

Suddenly I felt cool and quiet inside myself.

"I'm sorry, Dessi. But, like you, I'm busy. And I'll admit that unless there is a special reason, I don't make the effort to maintain contact," I replied, apologetically, but with no intention of seeming to beg for her forgiveness. "And if the police have called, well that is their job, looking at connections when someone is murdered."

I wasn't sure what to do next. I could forget what I had come for. Pretend to have only come for a social call. But I didn't think there was much point in doing that. Whatever family bond there had once seemed to be between us was obviously shallow and probably now gone and wasn't likely to ever be recovered in any meaningful way by begging her for anything.

"And you haven't made the effort either, Dessi. Not for a long time. So, we're even. I'm pleased Anoushka and Con have both done so well for themselves."

I paused, seeing that Dessi was looking at me as if she just wanted me out of her house, or dead. And I knew there was no point my being there. So I turned and headed to the front door, opening it myself.

On the doorstep I turned back to my cousin. "I'm sorry that it doesn't mean anything to you that your cousin Maria was murdered, Dessi. Or that she has been found at last. I missed your condolence call. The one I had expected when the papers were full of the story barely a couple of weeks ago. And I have never had anything against your father. If he was involved, I doubt he was doing more than trying to protect one of his family," I said to her calmly, as she stood rigidly in the hallway where I had left her. Then I closed the front door behind me.

I drove home in a state of aggressive concentration, unable to be sympathetic or understanding towards such narrow-minded blindness and stupidity. I was disgusted that my selfish father's death of old age would be sure to mean more to Dessi than whatever had happened to my sister Maria, her cousin.

When I got home I wanted to be able to release my anger by telling someone about my meeting with Dessi. I was still ready to explode about her behavior, but only the dogs were available, and they were unable to tell me how right I was to be angry. I looked at them, but they were only able to look concerned or sympathetic. And that was probably only my imagination giving them human qualities.

CHAPTER 17

The day after I went to Sydney to see Dessi I got a
phone call at home in the morning. Early. I was just out of bed
and almost didn't answer it. And when I did I didn't recognize
the voice of the man on the other end and got annoyed.

"Who is this?" I'd snapped irritably,

"It's Ray. Dessi's husband," the man replied.

"Oh. Oh," I said, hoping I wasn't going to get a round
of abuse for going to see his wife and upsetting her. "I had no
intention of upsetting Dessi, Ray," I got in quickly.

"I know, James. I know. But I'm afraid you can't even
hint at anything negative about her saintly brother or her father
without her going off the deep end."

"I noticed."

He paused before going on. "Anyway, last night she told
me about your visit, and I wanted to give you a call to see if I
can help. Rocky was a complete arsehole. And if he hadn't got
killed when he did, I probably wouldn't have married Dessi. But
don't ever tell her that. The thought of him treating my home
and everything in it like it was for his convenience, the way he
did his parent's house, just wasn't on. He was keeping drugs in
their big shed, you know. And moving stolen cars through the

warehouse and even the shed. But to the girls he was a saint, and they would give him anything he wanted. Lie for him, whatever."

I remembered the big shed Uncle Nick had behind their house. It had been his first freight depot, when he had gone from being just another Greek migrant driving a truck to being a freight carrier in his own right, with two trucks. And when I was a child the shed had seemed to me to be the biggest place ever built. Until I had later seen the warehouse.

Now I wasn't sure what to say to Ray. I had never had much to do with him, and his call had caught me completely by surprise. I had never talked about the real Rocky to anyone either. Deep down there was a part of me that was still the young boy who had idolized him and wanted him to be what I had once imagined, and Dessi still did imagine—even while the adult me knew he wasn't.

"How did you know what was going on? Did you really know what Rocky was doing?" I asked, being cautious.

"Everybody except his family knew. He thought he was above the law, and he was dangerous. He didn't try to hide it from anyone who was frightened of him. And everyone who knew him was. Except his family, of course. They worshipped him. And he lied to them to keep them happy."

"Is that why Eudoxia and Anna ended up in Perth?" was all I could think to say. They had married brothers.

Ray's obvious dislike for Rocky was unexpected, given Dessi's very obvious devotion to his memory.

"Yeah, The Riolli boys put up with the situation for a while. But then Rocky beat up that Italian girl and put her in hospital. After that they'd had enough. He had his sisters give him an alibi, and the Riollis nearly got dragged into it too. The local Italian community wasn't happy with them. So the boys decided to get out. The building game was picking up over West, and they had family there, so they just went. That was what I wanted to tell you about James—the girls he beat up."

"I never heard about that," I said, not counting my mother's ramblings. "I was a bit young and my mother would go on about him sometimes, but I never really knew what happened." It wasn't the time to say that back then I had worshipped Rocky too.

"I'm not surprised. I only knew because he tried to drag me in as a witness. It was when I was first going out with Dessi. Probably about the time your sister went missing. And I didn't even have any idea what he was really like yet, because I only heard the wonderful things she said about him. But I wasn't going to lie to the police for him, though she did. And I didn't stop her. We were out together that particular night, so I knew she definitely wasn't home all evening. And when I had picked her up from her house, only her parents were at home. So I know the girls all lied. And his parents."

"I'm sorry," I said.

I'd known the family was close, but it hadn't really sunk in before just how tight they actually were.

"Did Dessi tell you Maria was found in a wooden crate like the ones her father used to ship up to Broken Hill?" I asked.

"Yes, I heard, after the police called Dessi. I wondered about that too. Dessi said that you came to accuse her father and brother of murdering your sister."

"No. Not at all," I replied, in surprise.

"Hey. I know. Don't worry. I know who you were thinking of, mate."

"If I thought anyone was involved, I thought it was more likely to be Rocky or my father. I know they were a close family; I could see Nick hiding her body for either of them. To protect them. Even my father. It wouldn't be the first time a man killed his daughter."

I hesitated a moment before I went on. I wasn't normally a man who revealed personal things to strangers. And I hadn't seen Ray for years.

"They used to argue a lot. My father and Maria. And I have wondered if it might have been accidental. Part of some argument . . ." I trailed off, hearing just how melodramatic the possibility sounded when spoken out loud. "Anyway, who was the girl you mentioned, that he'd beaten up? What happened? Do you know?"

"She was an Italian girl he went out with a few times. I have no idea now what her name was. The day after it happened the police arrived on his parents' doorstep. She was in hospital, saying Rocky raped her and beat her up because she wouldn't sleep with one of his mates. Fortunately, her family weren't that good. And Rocky's sisters and his parents were all saying he was with them the whole evening. No one else dared to back up her story. They were all either his mates or too scared of him. Shit, I was afraid of him. So nothing ever happened."

"Do you know for sure that he did it?"

"Yes. Definitely," Ray said forcefully. "The bastard told me later that he had. Said he'd beaten up lots of women and it was the only thing sluts understood if they didn't do what you wanted them to. Then he said I would need something more permanent than a hospital bed if I said anything about it to anyone."

"Fortunately, he died a year or so later. The only favor he ever did the world. Then it nearly made me sick the way Dessi and the rest carried on, wailing and weeping at the funeral," he added, then stopped. His anger was palpable even over the phone. "Anyway, I've got work to do, James. Sorry I can't tell you any more. But I'd just not long met Dessi and her family when your sister disappeared, and I really didn't think much about it. I mean we didn't even know for sure she was dead. At that age . . ." he trailed off, being honest.

"Do you know if Rocky had anything to do with her, with my sister?"

"Sorry. No. Rocky had plenty of women after him here. He was good-looking and had a way with him. I don't know really, but I can't see him going up to Moorebank to see any girl."

I thanked him for his call and wondered how his sisters could have been so blind and obsessed as to lie for Rocky about something so serious—especially about him beating up another young woman.

Ray's phone call also made me realize that if Rocky had anything to do with Maria I was very unlikely to ever find it out from any of his sisters, which meant I wasn't likely to find it out.

But I was wrong. Time and life had changed the sisters too.

Dessi's sister, Eudoxia, called me from Perth the next day.

CHAPTER 18

"Eudoxia, here, James," she said. "Dessi called me today, and, well, I had to call you. I am so sorry, James. I hadn't heard, honestly. Not till today. I am so sorry about Maria."

"Thank you," I said, surprised. "It's been a shock. I am—"

"I can imagine. And I am sorry about Dessi. She is still living in a fairyland where everyone in the family was perfect." She paused for breath, "Unfortunately, she married a good husband and has two perfect children. So she has never had to come to terms with reality."

"I have a good husband too, just not perfect children," she said with a laugh and then paused. "Our young Tony is very like Rocky. It took us a while to accept what he was like. Me longest. It's not easy, James. I know that. You want your kids to be perfect. But I don't think that parents are so naïve today. And my dad was a peasant at heart, I don't mean that negatively. Just that his only son was the most important person in the world to him. And he had to believe Rocky was going to make him proud. Your dad didn't seem to be like that, and it's not so common now," she added, and I had to agree.

But then I hadn't ever been a handsome, smiling, confident young god like Rocky.

"Do you know if there was anything between him and Maria?" I asked.

"She had a big crush on him for a while. But Rocky wasn't stupid; he knew he would be pushing it if your dad or ours found out there was anything going on between them. And he had his choice of girls. Rocky was clever; he knew how to spin a good story. He was a very good liar, just like my Tony is. Good liars and good looking. It will help them to get away with a lot, James. But they often know just how far they can go too, and when it's not worth the trouble."

She continued. "But I am not calling you to tell you about my problems. I was calling . . . damn," she said.

I had heard the sound of door chimes in the background.

"Just a minute while I see who it is," she said, and I heard footsteps retreating. Then voices, blurred and shifting. Then footsteps returning.

"I'm sorry. I have to go, James. I will call you later. Sorry. Bye." She sounded flat suddenly, and I was cut off before I'd even said my own good-bye.

It was interesting to see how the sisters had changed. And I wondered how bad her son really was, I seemed to remember she had two boys and a girl. But I was not certain and could not have told you their names. Her call made me feel even more guilty about how much I had let my family contacts slip.

CHAPTER 19

After talking to Ray and Eudoxia I knew that I wanted to visit my father, and that I had to, because there were too many things unsaid between us. But it certainly wasn't a visit I was looking forward to. Unfortunately, I also knew that putting it off would just make it harder. So, on Saturday morning I called him to arrange it.

I picked up the phone and dialed, glad it only rang twice before it was answered. If he was sitting next to the phone, he let it ring twice on principle. It satisfied some law. If it rang more than twice, it meant he'd had to get to it, which always made him irritable, or he was out.

"Yes?" his gravelly voice barked at the other end.

"Hello, Dad. It's me, James," I replied.

"So, when are you coming to visit me? Ken died last week. He was my best mate here. Did you know that? Poor bastard dropped dead on his way to lunch. Right in the middle of the hallway. In front of the old ladies. Dead before he hit the floor, they reckon. Terrible."

He didn't seem to remember that he had already told me this story last time I had spoken to him. I wondered if he was starting to lose it. Or if he just didn't care if he had repeated it or not.

"I'm sorry to hear that, Dad," I replied uncertainly, "So how's the food?"

"Lousy, like always. So, what you calling for?"

"I wanted to come by today. Will that be OK?"

There was a pause. "Sure. But I'm busy, so come before lunch," he requested grudgingly and then hung up before I could say anything.

Too bad if I couldn't have left straight away.

My drive to Gosford was done in lovely sunshine, but there was a chilly breeze. It was a deceptive day. When you were inside, you thought how lovely it looked outside, but when you went out, you quickly realized there was little warmth in the sun—certainly not enough to make up for the cold breeze blowing in off the ocean.

My father had lived at the Mountain Views retirement home in Primalta for the last twelve years. Ever since his sister Effie—Ephonia—had died. It was a large retirement complex but had always seemed to be a very well-run place, and the staff were considerate and reliable. Compared to some of the retirement homes I had heard of, his was a paradise.

Aunt Effie and I had never got along. Though the dislike, or whatever it had been, had all been on her side.

She had not encouraged my father and me to keep in touch. So, once he had left my mother and gone to the Central Coast to live with his sister, I rarely saw my father.

He had arranged to meet me on a couple of my birthdays. We had met in a park, and I had sat there nervously, while he seemed to ignore me. They had been short visits. And each time he had given me a present that related to soccer. Once it was a French national team shirt, another time a pair of Brazilian team shorts. They had both been too big for me. I had never even grown to be the size he wanted, he had been a big man and very tall, but even now I was only medium, in height and size.

Whenever I had looked at myself when I was a teenager, I had been disappointed. I had wanted to be thin and tall. Even androgynous looking, like the rock stars of the time. Like David Bowie. Instead, I had been too well-built and not tall enough.

At twenty-one I had escaped from my mother and gone to Darwin to work, and at twenty-six I had returned to help care for my mother and made a serious effort to get to know my father.

It had often taken several calls before Effie and I were finally able to settle on a suitable time and date for a visit. And even then she hovered about, frowning at me, as if I was some unpleasant stranger who had wandered in off the street, trying to sell them something, rather than my father's only child and her nephew. And she would hurry me off as quickly as she felt was polite, which my father had never seemed to mind.

Once he had moved into the retirement home it had become easier. And since then I saw him regularly once a month. When Allison and I were married, she had gone along also and he had taken to her from the start. Our regular visits had become ones where I made the strong Turkish coffee he liked and then sat back, waiting until it was time to tidy up, while Allison and my father talked endlessly, laughed often, and flirted mildly.

Allison had made an effort to get on with both my parents and had succeeded. Not an easy task.

No. Not an easy task at all.

CHAPTER 20

Allison had tried hard to please us all. Too hard.

Two days after the papers carried the news about Maria being found Allison rang me.

Allison's voice on the phone brought back a flood of images and emotions. I was too stunned at hearing it to know what to say. I discovered she was still in Germany and that the German tourist, who had been sixteen years older than her, had died of a heart attack some months before. She was coming home in a matter of days, bringing her son with her, and not sure for how long.

I said, "Yes. Do. Call me when you get here. Come around."

"My mother told me you had built your house."

"Did she? Yes, yes I have."

"She says it's very modern."

"Oh."

"I don't think she likes it," Allison added, and I could hear amusement in her voice.

After all those years I recognized her amusement. It was as if I had heard it last only moments before. She was so achingly familiar.

On the Sunday after I visited Dessi, Allison called me from her parent's home.

I was again caught out by the familiarity of her. Her voice, even with its overlay of a slight German accent. Her way of saying things.

Her parents were taking her son out for the day, to the beach, and she was free.

"I'd like to see you," I said, without even thinking about it.

"You are sure?" she asked.

"Yes." I had no doubts. "Come over. I'd like to see you. Do you need to be picked up?" I asked her, suddenly thinking of her alone in her parent's house at Coal Point with no transport.

"No," she said. "No, James, I'm fine. I have Dad's car. How about we meet at the Jetty Club?" she said.

She was telling me. It was not like her to be so decisive. It surprised me, and it made me nervous. I wondered in how many other ways she had changed in the intervening years.

I arrived early and found a table outside but worried that Allison might not want to sit there. I didn't even order a coffee while I waited, not wanting her to feel we couldn't change tables. The old Allison would have asked me where I wanted to go and then let me choose the table. I was not sure about the new one.

The old Allison had tried hard to make our marriage work. Too hard. After the first excitement of living with her I had needed to have time alone. I know now that there had been things I had needed to work through. But she had felt that my need to get away from her meant she must be doing something wrong. So she had tried harder to please me. And when that hadn't worked, she had tried even harder.

But the harder she had tried the guiltier I had felt about needing to get away from her. And the more I had needed to get away from her. She thought that more sex would help and threw herself at me. Tried to surprise me, arouse me, but often it did the opposite. I already felt confused about how I felt when we made love and I needed time to adjust, to grow up. I hadn't needed her to be more provocative, more demanding.

Odd thing to say, I know. But that was it. The sex, and how I had felt about it, had often left me feeling guilty and wicked. More sex, more guilt. Like her, I had also felt pushed into a corner, where nothing I did was right.

In the end nothing either of us did was right.

We rarely talked about what we felt, which may or may not have helped. Instead, we moved on to blaming each other, and now I had to admit that I had been at fault, or at least the main cause of our problems. But it wasn't a fault I could have remedied overnight, or under pressure, back when we had been married. And it might be a fault I could never really remedy.

I didn't know her father's car, but I was watching each one that pulled in nearby. I first saw her when she got out of one that had parked on the opposite side of the road and then turned toward me. My gut turned over. She had changed, but she hadn't changed. Whatever I had seen in her in the beginning I saw now. I recognized the way she turned and moved before I recognized her face. As she got closer, I recognized her shy smile before her face even came together for me. She had changed her hair. She was in jeans and a T-shirt. Plain, simple. The green of the T-shirt perfectly set off her coloring, her auburn hair, her pale skin.

I stood up and smiled nervously. I had surprisingly discovered that she still attracted me.

She stopped on the other side of the table, not coming closer.

"We can move," I said nervously, "Go to another table."

"No. This is fine," she replied, taking her seat as I sat back down.

"So . . . you're looking well," I said, meaning it. She looked more than well. She glowed; she was not the worried, hurt, and angry woman I had last seen her as.

We talked of nothings, maneuvering to get a feel for each other. Nervous of opening old hurts. I asked about her son.

"His name's Wolfy, James. Well really it's Wolfgang, after his grandfather. He's six years old."

She told me that he missed his father but that he was too young to really understand. Old enough to miss him, but not old enough to understand fully what had happened.

It seemed odd to be there like that. I found that I still thought of the woman sitting opposite me as mine, yet we were talking about her having another man's child.

Allison had been very good with my dogs; she had taken to them and them to her. We had decided to try dog showing, and she and got heavily involved with that. She had attacked it with the same dedication she gave to everything she took up, like our marriage, my parents, the German, Asia.

Now, at a distance of many years and with the wisdom I had acquired during those years I could see the relationship between us as I hadn't been able to back then. Now I felt sorry for the unpleasantness there had been between us, and I hoped she had been happy with the German. She had certainly deserved to be.

The dogs had never looked so well groomed once she had gone and I had quickly lost interest in showing them. Now they just occupied the house and provided company for me.

"Children need two parents," I said.

"Yes, they do," she replied. "How is your father?"

"The same," I said. "The same."

I had no desire to discuss him.

"And how does he feel about Maria being found?" she asked.

It was a natural question, of course. But I had no acceptable answer ready for her and I looked down at the table and fiddled with my coffee cup as I waited for inspiration.

"He hung up on me when I phoned to tell him. But it was in the papers, and you know he gets all the papers," I said finally, not seeing any reason not to tell her the truth.

Allison had liked my father and got on well with him. Better than I ever had.

"Oh. I'm sorry," she replied, then confused me again by adding, "I'm surprised you think a child is better off with two parents, James. Neither of yours were easy."

I shrugged, annoyed for some reason. "You seemed to get on well with both of them."

"I tried hard to. Family is important to me. But I could see that they were both very difficult. And now that I'm older and have a son of my own, I think that they were both too self-centered to ever be good parents. And what happened, Maria's disappearance, was too much for both of them."

I was surprised. I also wanted to change the subject.

"How long are you staying in Australia?"

She looked at me seriously, with her thinking look. And I almost laughed. But instead I sat back and waited for . . . probably for something about why things hadn't worked out between us. The chemistry was obviously there still.

"Do you still wear that skirt, James?" she asked quietly. "The white vinyl one?"

I went cold. I wanted to get up and leave. Just walk out. Leave her there. But I was frozen in my chair, staring at the lake. I couldn't look at her. I wanted to kill her.

CHAPTER 21

The Mountain Views retirement village has a well-ordered village atmosphere. Tidy small home units line the narrow roads that wind about the complex, finally leading to the main accommodation and office building.

I had driven in carefully and slowly; the winding roads were quaint but made driving hazardous. They were so narrow there were no footpaths on some of the streets, and the curves occasionally hid elderly residents tottering along the side of the road on their walkers. But I arrived safely and parked in the car park outside the building where my father lived. It houses forty single-resident studio units, a communal dining and games room, the kitchens, and the offices where the complexes administration staff work.

Behind this building is the larger "end of life" center that houses those no longer able to care for themselves, including the dementia sufferers. They keep the doors locked on that wing, and the only time I had gone inside I had felt as much as if I were entering a prison as a nursing center. I'd had to press the buzzer by the door and wait to be admitted, and do the same to leave.

There is death, and there is being dead, I had thought, and shuddered. Maria's death was at least clean in that way.

When he'd moved in, my father could have bought his own small home unit on one of the narrow winding roads. He'd certainly been healthy and mobile enough. But he didn't want to be bothered with cooking for himself or gardening, so he had gone directly into one of the self-contained studios. Even now that he was fifteen years older he was still the odd one out there. All the other rooms in his wing continued to be occupied by people who were far less active and much frailer than he was, and there were few other men.

I walked through the foyer into the wide passageway that ran the length of the building. There was a motorized scooter parked outside one of the resident's doors, and some of the wooden doors had fancy little name plaques hanging on them. Those doors always seemed to me to be ones where people wanted to cry out to passers-by that inside someone was still alive, and still had an identity. Still had a desire to be known and recognized as a special individual.

To me, they were sadder doors than the anonymous ones, which I passed, like my father's. Doors with nothing but the institutional brass room number on them. Somehow those other, marked doors, were doors for people whose bodies had failed too long before their spirit had.

I knocked on the plain door of room 17, and a barked "Come in" summoned me to enter.

Inside the studio my father had every comfort. There was an enormous television, which was always on. Not, thank god, blaring like Frank, the frozen man's. He also had a stereo and a video machine, but his pride was the enormous, electrically operated recliner chair in the center of the room. There were remote controls for everything. He always kept them lined up in the correct order on a special table that was beside him.

The television sat in the center of a long, deep, dresser covered with pictures of his family. They were mostly of himself and his brothers as young men. All good-looking. All dark haired, tall, and muscular. Several of them in their swimsuits, standing alone or in laughing groups on some Sydney beach. Then there were others of the brothers as they grew older, often posing with their families. And then there were some pictures of their children, my father's nephews and nieces, alone, at their graduations or weddings. There was only one picture of me, his son. It was hidden well back behind larger photos of Uncle Nick and his smiling, good-looking son, Rocky, and his three girls.

There were no pictures of Maria. As far as I knew our father had never had a photo of her. I knew that but didn't understand it. There was, of course, no photo of my mother. Or of us as a family. Their separation had been acrimonious from the start, and their divorce had only made things even more bitter between them.

No wonder he wasn't keen on his children, I vaguely thought. But of course the divorce had come later. He had already moved away from us emotionally long before the physical or legal parting had occurred.

Hanging on his walls were my father's greatest treasures—the elaborately framed autographed photos of famous soccer players that he had collected over his lifetime. In his youth my father had played soccer well, and in his old age he had again become passionate about the game, even going to the World Cup when it had been in Italy in 1990. He had planned to go to Germany for 2006, but it hadn't happened. But he still talked of going again.

I had no idea what his financial situation was. He had plenty of gadgets, still had a car, and lived comfortably, but he spent very little on anything else. For all I knew he might have almost nothing in the bank or have a small fortune. Whatever his situation, I had no doubt he would never ask me for any help if he needed it, and when I had once been asked what I thought he would leave me when he died, I had answered, "Nothing."

"So you made it. You look all right, not sick." My father greeted me. Saying what he always did, and not bothering to get up from his recliner. "Make us a coffee. So, how you been? You haven't had trouble at work, have you?" he asked me as I went through into the tiny kitchenette that was tucked into a corner, next to the much bigger bathroom.

Meals for those living in the studios were served in the dining room at the end of the hallway, but in these old units the small kitchen made them very independent.

I automatically put on the kettle and got out the cups and saucers and started to make the coffee. He liked thick, dark Turkish-style coffee. I would boil the water in the electric jug while I spooned the finely ground coffee into the special pot. Then once the water had boiled I would pour it over the grounds in the pot and bring it back to the boil on the small stove. When the coffee began to bubble, I would take it off and put it to stand and settle for a few minutes so that the grounds didn't go into the cups when I carefully poured it out.

He always had fresh drinking water in a long glass beside him.

"Good for the kidneys," he would rumble.

For him, coffee was "bad for the kidneys" and water was good. He'd complain about how he'd get a pain in the kidneys if he drank too much of the strong Turkish coffee he insisted on.

"Do you want a biscuit?" I called out, looking into the cupboard to see what was there.

"Of course. There are some chocolate ones."

My father liked to have them put out on a plate, like his sister, Effie, used to do for him when he lived with her. For how long, I wondered, as I opened the packet and set out five biscuits on the small plate. Over twenty years, I realized now that I actually thought about it.

He had lived with his sister, Effie, for longer than he had lived with his own mother, or even with his wife, my mother. Which I thought made my father's sister more like his wife than his wife had been. And I realized for the first time that not only had my Aunt Effie never made any attempt to maintain contact between my father and me, but she had also never made any mention of my sister, or done anything to remind him of her existence.

Perhaps it was her fault, not my father's, that there had been so little contact between us after he left. But after so long I knew it didn't matter any more who had caused the situation. And my father had been an adult; he'd always had a choice.

89

I brought the coffees in and put them and the biscuits beside the remotes on the small table next to him. Then I sat down myself on the only other chair in the room, a straight-backed one with a padded tapestry covered seat and wooden arms.

"You're looking good," I said nervously. "Are you sleeping well?"

He shrugged, still watching the television, even though the sound was muted.

"Not last night. Dan, my neighbor, he died last night," he said, sounding annoyed. "They found him on the floor this morning. Cold. I got woken up in the night by noises. Banging. From there," he said, indicating the room to the left of his by a shake of his solid head. "Must have been him falling about."

I was silent for a moment, taken aback by the awfulness of the image of Dan, who I had met a couple of times, floundering about in death. Dan had been a frail, quiet man, always polite. When he did talk, he was obviously still alert and intelligent, and much more aware of current happenings in politics than I was. He had once been a tall man, but in old age he had curled over as if he had been listening to short people for too long.

"Did you call the nurse?" I asked my father.

"No. Why? Some noise woke me up. So? I was tired. Often I wake up. How should I know what was going on with him. I just hear banging, and go back to sleep when it stops."

I couldn't think of anything to say. My father showed no concern for what had happened, for whether he could have done anything.

"Have you spoken to Dessi recently?" I asked finally.

There was a short silence, "She's a good girl, rings me every week. Two beautiful children. Both successful. Why don't you have children? Time you found another woman. You be lucky to find another as good as that Allison. What did she marry you for anyway if you give her no kids?"

It was part of his regular rant, and I had learned to ignore it. But today it irritated me and I couldn't just brush it off, because his obvious self-centeredness and lack of concern for others, even for Dan, his neighbor and supposed friend, had made me angry with him.

"Dessi wasn't happy to speak to me when I went down to Sydney to see her. I doubt she will be coming to Maria's funeral."

There was a long pause as my father fiddled with his remotes, moving them about on the small table, and flipping through the channels on the TV.

"Why should we go? Any of us?" he suddenly rumbled angrily. "She was nothing to do with us. She never listened to me. She was not my daughter."

My father was working his mouth the way he did when he was really annoyed and liable to explode into a rage. But I was too shocked by what he had said to think about that just then.

"Maria was your daughter. Why say she wasn't? She was my sister," I answered back.

He turned and glared angrily at me, stabbing the air with his right hand in what could have been a rude gesture.

"Ha, what do you know? You know how long we were married when she was born? Your mother was a slut, her daughter was a slut, and you . . ." he trailed off angrily, looking away again.

I was lost. I didn't know how long after they were married Maria had been born. It wasn't the sort of thing I would ever have thought of looking into. I had no idea even exactly when my parents were married. It threw me briefly. If he really did think she wasn't his daughter then maybe there was some reason for how he had behaved, even if it was a bad one.

"You raised her as your daughter," was all I could say.

"So, I was a fool. But now I am not a fool," he replied loudly and proudly.

I knew my father would have known everything that was reported on TV or in the papers about Maria's discovery. There were two papers there even then, lying on the floor beside his recliner. And I was suddenly past caring what he thought.

"She was your daughter. And you would have read about Broken Hill in the paper, Dad, but not about the box she was found in. It was like the ones Nick's trucks took up there. So, do you know what happened to her, if Rocky had anything to do with Maria?" It was the killer question but I didn't care.

There was another extended silence until my father finally exploded and turned on me.

"You never talk about any one in my family like that! In the same breath as you talk about that slut who was out any chance she got! My family worked hard; my brother Nicki was a saint. He raised four beautiful kids! Those girls got good husbands. Good kids."

My father picked up the plate of biscuits and threw the lot at me, the plate and the biscuits all missing and falling to the floor as his electric lift recliner started humming.

The big chair was righting itself ponderously while my father flailed about angrily, yelling and trying to lever himself up out of the chair before it was upright enough.

"You shit bastard, how dare you bother Dessi. You are no son of mine! She was no daughter, and you, . . .you were never a son. Get out of here. Get out, you poofter bastard! I know why you don't have kids; you think I'm stupid?"

"Maria was your daughter, Dad, and she was murdered. Doesn't that mean anything to you? Did you do it? Did Rocky?" I yelled angrily back at him. "She has been found where Uncle Nick used to go with his truck, in a box just like he used to carry. Did you kill her, Dad? Have an argument like you were always having with her and do it accidentally? Get Nick, or Evan, to hide her so no one knew? Is that what happened?" I was yelling at my father, furious, letting it all pour out.

"Or was it Rocky. Did he do it? Are you all protecting him still?"

I stopped yelling and found myself panting and shaking with anger as the electric recliner finally righted itself, and my father began pushing himself out of it.

"You poofter shit, you are no son of mine! Fuck off!" my father shouted as he finally stood up and began lumbering across the few feet of floor that lay between us.

His expression was one of uncontrollable fury, his face red, his fists clenched, and his head pushed forward like a battering ram. And I had no intention of seeing how strong he

92

still was. I turned and left the room, with his continuing abuse being bellowed after me.

I strode down the passageway, away from him, and he followed me briefly before returning to his studio and slamming the door violently.

A little old lady peered tentatively around the last, partly opened studio door in the corridor, and I forced a smile out for her. She smiled politely back and disappeared, closing the door with a sharp click. I knew I had handled things worse than badly, but in a way it was a relief to accuse him at last of what I had been wondering about ever since I had heard where Maria had been found.

As I left the building and drove home I accepted that there were bridges in life that got burned because they serve no purpose any more. Led to nothing. And I accepted that the relationship I had tried to build with my father was now just one of those.

CHAPTER 22

The next day I bought the paper on the way to work and discovered the headlines were all about a schoolgirl whose body had been found hidden under the heavy leaf litter beneath the Jacarandas in Sydney's Hyde Park. She had been discovered early the previous night, just in time to make the morning headlines.

And even though I knew it was understandable, I suddenly felt angry that the police would be far more concerned with solving this new murder than with worrying about another teenage girl in a school uniform killed over thirty years before.

I hadn't heard anything more from the police about their investigation into Maria's death since the brief conversation I'd had on the phone with some detective. Wright, David Wright, I seemed to remember had been his name. It had been the day after I was told Maria had been found.

The newly dead girl, whose name hadn't been released yet, was also seventeen and also wearing her school uniform and on her way home from school when she had disappeared.

For a moment my heart dropped at the thought there might be some connection with Maria's death. That it wasn't family, or some friend, after all, but instead some psychopath who had picked her up randomly and who, after all these years had done it again. And another part of me thought, good, that meant that now the police would find him quickly and easily and he'd be punished at last.

But then I had to stop reading when I thought about how her parents must feel. And I knew they wouldn't understand it if I told them that they were lucky to know where their daughter was. The not knowing eroded the soul over the years. I knew that, the not knowing.

I had no idea what my father truly felt now. After the scene at the home I could only wonder if he had in the end somehow come to terms with her disappearance by convincing himself it was "right." Some judgment from God for her willfulness, her argumentativeness. I doubted that was what he had thought in the beginning. I doubted it but could never know for sure. But I also knew that my father was a man of black-and-white views who would probably not choose to remember that he had once felt differently.

Was Maria's killer a woman or a man, I'd wondered briefly when I first heard she was found. I'd have said a man. It was what my mother had always implied, what I had thought, what everyone thought, but it was possible it wasn't. But only barely. And I'd briefly wondered too if her killer might even come to her funeral. If he might be there somewhere, sitting in the crowd. And I had laughed at the possibility. Then I had known it was possible. It was a small town, and if it wasn't Rocky who had killed her, then it was some other family member or friend of hers, and it would be natural and expected for them to be there.

But if her killer had died? Then they would have escaped his punishment forever. And I didn't want to accept that. It was depressing unless you believed in a hell. Which I didn't.

And I knew that it was us, her family, who had suffered all these years. Who had gone to hell.

Keith's hand touching my arm jerked me back into the present.

"They are ready for you. A bit early I'm afraid. Are you right to see them now?"

"Oh. Who?" I asked blankly, I had been completely tied up in my thoughts before he interrupted me.

"The television people. And the local paper. They are ready to ask a few questions and take a few photos, " Keith replied patiently.

I looked about, straightened my tie, and pulled myself together. The newly murdered schoolgirl had at least taken the Sydney media's attention away from Maria.

CHAPTER 23

One evening Jennifer Toomey had called me. I recognized her voice immediately. She wanted me to know that she had finally caught up with Pat and that they had talked about Maria, as she had said they probably would.

"Pat would like to meet you, James," she told me. "I think she knows a bit more than she told the police, but she seems frightened of talking to them. She said she would talk to you, though."

"When?" I blurted out. "When can I meet her?"

"I said I would organize dinner at my place. Is that all right with you? Pat worried me. She wasn't her usual self at all. She says it's been preying on her mind ever since they found Maria's body." Jennifer hesitated for a moment "You will be all right with this, won't you, James?" she asked.

"What do you mean?" I asked.

"If she tells you something you think is important, but she doesn't want to go to the police with it, you will understand, won't you?"

I stopped for a moment, and thought. "Yes, I promise I won't be angry with her," I said, understanding. "But I won't promise not to tell the police myself," I added, wondering how I could do that without dragging Pat into things.

Jennifer was silent for a short while, and I wondered if I had made a big mistake by telling her the truth. I wanted desperately to hear what Pat had to say.

"I will have to tell her that, James, when I get back to her. If it's OK, is Thursday night good for you?"

Thursday was agreed, but I was uncertain if it would happen. I had no idea now if Pat would still be willing to meet me. But Jennifer must have been reasonably confident that it would go ahead, as she gave me the directions to her apartment on the lakefront. I didn't know the building she was in, but I knew the road, and I knew that she had to be doing well in the real estate business if she could afford to live there.

* * * *

The same night my cousin, Linda—good, reliable Linda, who I rarely saw, had called me again. She had called me as soon as she heard about Maria being found but was calling again now the other calls had dried up.

She was checking to make sure I was still OK, and I was surprised and appreciated her thoughtfulness in calling again so soon, as we rarely saw or spoke to each other.

Nothing deliberate, it was just the way things happened. I only ever went to Rose's house for Christmas, or to sit outside and wait to pick her up, and I wasn't into children's birthday parties, which were about the only other family gatherings that occurred.

"I'm going fine," I told her.

"Good," she said, "I know everyone checks up on you just after something bad happens, but it's often a couple of weeks later that people suddenly feel lost and most appreciate a call. I learnt that in my course," she said.

"Oh. Which course is that?" I asked, not aware she was doing anything in particular, apart from working in the family business, a cleaning business, and looking after two young children.

"Nursing. I'm studying nursing. Well, assistant in nursing. I have a bit of time, and I figure it'll help if I ever have my parents and Cicely to look after."

"Will you be able to pay for some help?" I asked. "Has Cicely still got her share of the money that grandma Flynn left? That will help won't it?"

Rose and Frank led a quiet life. Cicely was on a pension, Rose got a pension as her carer, and of course Frank worked. The pensions were not huge, I knew, but added together it had to be a reasonable amount. From Rose's conversation, money wasn't short, but she was careful with it, which made a difference. They seemed to have whatever they wanted, including two nearly new cars. And she was proud to let everyone know that they didn't owe anything and owned their house and the cars.

"That money? You didn't know? No. You were in Darwin then, I think. When we each turned eighteen and were able to get our share of the money, Mum got it all. It's how they bought the house they have now. I know you get on well with my mother, James, but she can be very determined and forceful."

"Oh," I said, surprised, but mainly making conversation. "No, I didn't know. What happened?"

"Mum knew she could have Cicely's share when the time came, but that wasn't enough to do what she wanted to do. So, she convinced me it would be best to give her what was coming to me too. After all, I would be living in the house for a few years until I got married, she said. And later I'd get it anyway when I cared for Cicely after she was gone. Mum felt she and Cicely were entitled to live comfortably if she was going to be looking after Cicely the rest of her life and that I should put Cicely and her first also. As she pointed out at the time, I will inherit everything eventually. Or my children will, so the money will come back to me, and the house will be worth a lot more when it does.

"Of course she didn't say anything about me inheriting Cicely too. But I already knew I was," she added.

"So, how did you feel about that? Or rather how do you feel about that? I only found out the other day that your mother thinks I should help you if you need it."

"I was brought up expecting I would, James, so for years I automatically assumed I would. And I have no doubt my mother has things tied up so I will inherit nothing if I don't. She said as much recently, when Lyle and I told her we were thinking about moving further into the Hunter Valley and opening a B&B once the kids leave school. Once she was diagnosed I always came second to Cicely when we were growing up. And to be honest, there are times now when I feel that we are doing just fine, so if the money is tied to Cicely and she can be looked after by someone else, or put into a good home then when the time comes, we may be quite happy with that." After saying this, Linda hesitated and then continued. "I know you get on well with Mum, so please don't say anything. And I know what she expects; she was also saying the other day that it's lucky you have no children so we can share the load."

"Yes, I gather she expects me to help care for Cicely, But I am not sure it will happen. How does she expect me to, anyway?"

"However you can, James. I honestly don't know what I will do when the time comes. But I'm afraid I am not going to make everyone else in my family take second place to Cicely the way my mother has. Particularly my dad. But please don't tell my mother that. She would make our lives hell," she added.

"No," I said, "I wouldn't."

I had only just started to realize how much of Linda's mother's life, Rose's life, revolved around Cicely, and I found it rather disturbing.

"If I were you I would probably also see about arranging for Cicely to go into some sort of a home," I told her honestly, "But then Cicely isn't my sister," I added, not knowing how I would really feel.

"We probably will. Its my dad I really feel really sorry for," Linda replied with sudden vehemence. "He has given up everything to do what Mum decided was best. It makes me angry sometimes. She has changed him and not in good ways. He was very good looking when they got married and had quite a reputation as a ladies man, and she wanted to settle him down, I think. But what she has done is to make him a slave to her and Cicely."

"Frank was a ladies man?"

"Yes. Played up a few times not long after they were married too, I gather."

"Well, he must have been different back then."

"Yes, he was. I can remember when he was always laughing and happy. My mother too. I think they were very happy when they were first married. Then once Cicely was diagnosed things seem to have gone wrong. I don't know why. But my mother decided he was irresponsible, and she took control of all the decisions. And then soon everything had to be done for Cicely's welfare."

My father just became a yes man. Withdrew into himself and lost interest. Why he just took it I don't know. Which annoys me too. That he didn't fight back. My mother even made him feel responsible for Cicely's problems."

"That's ridiculous. But I don't think your father likes me," I said, for no reason.

"I think he is just envious that you are so free, James," she replied. "I know he never talks to you, but he has said things. He felt sorry for you when you were young. Now he hates to be reminded of that time."

There wasn't really anything I could say to that. Families work in odd ways, and unless you are inside them you can never know what is going on.

"Anyway, I think I have told you enough about our problems for one day," she added. "And I didn't ring up for that. I'd better go. We'll see you at the funeral. But if you need any help, just call, OK?"

"OK," I answered, thinking how it is that death and funerals bring people back together. Like weddings. But we had been short on weddings.

The weddings in my family had all been years before, and the next lot weren't going to start for some years. I had an idea that Linda's eldest girl was about fifteen. My own wedding to

Allison had been low key. I had got into a temper with the planning and started saying, "If it is going to be this complicated and expensive, I am starting to wonder if it's worth it." And Allison had given in and not had the wedding she really wanted.

I had never really thought about Rose's devotion to Cicely before. I pretty much ignored Cicely if I could, and was just grateful that Rose handled her so well. But now I realized that Cicely went everywhere with her, except to do the shopping. And I did not remember Rose and Frank ever even having a holiday alone together.

CHAPTER 24

There were a lot of things I had not got around to asking Rose about when I'd had dinner with her. This partly was because of the shock I had when Rose told me how Maria had come by the large amount of money that had been lying in her bankbook for thirty years. Now I needed to know more. So I phoned her as I was leaving the office one afternoon.

"Rose," I said, "Can we talk. I—"

"James, not now. I'll call you back," she said sharply and hung up.

It wasn't like Rose to be flustered.

It was odd but I had other things to think of and to do, and she called me back on my mobile before I had time to worry too much about it. And what I had been busy with in the time between was doing research.

Up till then I had avoided reading any of the newspaper reports about Maria's discovery, but now I wanted information. And it was information that they might have printed. So I had gone straight from the office to the local library, where I knew they kept not only the local paper but also all of the major Sydney papers. I pulled out every edition printed in the ten days following the first announcement that Maria's body had been found, and spread them out on a table in the reference area. Then I set my mobile phone down next to me in case Rose called me back and started going through them.

What I was looking for was anything they had printed about the circumstances of Maria's original disappearance. When, where, and any possible suggestions of how or why. The names of people she had seen. That sort of thing. After an hour, I was disappointed, as I found very few specific details.

There was a lot of wordage written to highlight the sensational and emotive aspects of the story, rather than going into any depth about the facts. I read repeatedly that Maria was a talented and beautiful teenager, one whom everyone had loved, and that she had had been going to go to teachers college the following year. She had been generous, helpful, dedicated to her studies and to her ambition to teach. She sounded like the perfect young woman, and she had been murdered. It made for a good story, and I still wasn't in any position to say that all of that may not have been true about her.

According to the papers, she had been on her way home from St Cecilia's when she disappeared, and that was one of the few things I already knew. And also according to the newspapers she always took the same train home, and that day she had been on the train with her friends as normal and she had got off with a school friend at Biraben station as she usually did, apparently. That was not our local station. Our station was Fassiglen, and I wondered why she went on for two more stops and then caught a train back. I felt it had to be significant.

She had caught the next train back to Fassiglen from Biraben that day, and that was the last time she had been seen by anyone. The police had made extensive enquiries, and there had been a thorough search of the bush land surrounding both stations, as well as the creek she would have walked past on her way from Fassiglen station to our home.

I had never caught the train much as a child, and my memories of Fassiglen back then were vague. I had never done any more than see Biraben station out of the train window as I passed through it. I left the library with a plan, but Rose called me just as I was getting into my car.

"What was it you rang about, James?" she asked me.

"I want to know what you remember about Maria disappearing. What happened; who saw her? That sort of thing. Can we meet, can you talk now?" I asked her.

"You'll have to come here, James," she said. "I can't sit on the phone, and I can't go out just now. Cicely isn't well." There was a brief pause, "And Frank's gone out."

Frank never went out. Well, it seemed as if he never did. I'd never heard of him going anywhere unless it fitted in with Rose's plans. I hesitated to ask what had happened and then it was too late to ask anything. She had hung up already.

I went straight over to her house, wondering on the twenty-minute drive just what was going on. And I admit I was also wondering if I was making a wasted trip, hoping that Rose remembered things that had happened over thirty years before. I had no idea how much she and Frank had even been involved in what followed Maria's disappearance.

Rose's home was an immaculate and spacious early 1980s brick house built on the lakefront. I noticed the trim was freshly painted. Last time I had been there, to pick Rose up and take her to something, a Christmas concert I vaguely remembered, the front door had been a pale yellow. Now it was mid blue. In the day Frank slept, watched TV, and did maintenance on the house. That was his entire life.

I knew I couldn't stand to live like that. For all his faults Frank's life was his family. He was either at work or at home, allowing Rose the opportunity to leave Cicely and do the shopping and other things she needed, or wanted, to do on her own, while Frank played babysitter. I knew she couldn't take Cicely shopping, Rose had told me several times what a disaster it always was.

I'd heard that Frank had once had the opportunity of a promotion to Sydney. But they couldn't afford to move closer as he would have had to work days, which would have caused problems, because Rose still worked part time then. So he'd refused it and stayed where he was. I had never heard of him complaining.

They had added another room and bathroom on to the back of the house when Cicely got older. Rose once said Cicely was easily upset by noise, and I had wondered how she coped with Frank's TV. But I had also heard her grunting and shouting when she was frustrated or moody, and I wondered if the noise was, in fact, hers, and it was the rest of the family who had needed to put some distance between them and her.

Rose let me in and hurried me to the dining room. "Make yourself a coffee, James. I'll just check on Cicely," she said, and disappeared.

The house was oddly silent without Frank and his blaring television.

"Where's Frank?" I asked when she came back.

"I've no idea. But he shouted, and it upset Cicely. Shouted at me. After all I have had to put up with," she said angrily, shaking her head. I noticed her eyes were red rimmed, as if she had been crying. Rose never cried.

"Anyway, what was it you wanted to talk about? I heard that ex-wife of yours is in town. I hope she hasn't upset you. Don't let yourself get involved with her again; she's sure to be wanting someone to help with the boy she has now. She will take advantage of your easygoing nature, James, and you have enough to do already."

"No, that is not it," I said, surprised she had heard about Allison's arrival already. "No. Far from it. What I was curious about was what you knew or might have heard at the time Maria disappeared. What the local gossip was about what happened."

"They have found her now. Forget it. You know she is dead. Where she is. The funeral will be soon, and you can put it behind you."

"Just tell me," I said patiently.

Rose was obviously in a mood. Something she didn't get into often and something I had learned it was best to ignore when she did.

"What happened the day Maria didn't come home from school?" I asked, refusing to let it go.

"It's so long ago; does it matter?" she asked with some frustration.

"I need to know," I replied, pushing her.

She sat down, tiredly, like a heavy bag dropped onto the chair.

"Your mother was in a state that evening. She rang me. In a mess right from the start. But you know how she loved to be the center of attention. I was supposed to drop everything and go over. The next day Frank had to go into the station and ask the men on duty if anyone had seen Maria. He was having some time off. It was not long after we found out that Cicely was . . . was not well. Anyway, your mother had us running all over one side of town while she and your father ran about the rest of it, seeing Maria's friends and looking for her.

"I thought Maria was probably just staying out late with some friends or a boyfriend, but by midnight your parents had the police there. They said Maria wasn't one to not come home like that." Rose snorted. "She was allowed to do nearly whatever she wanted, so there was no need for her to cause trouble. But she liked to have her own way. Your father may have tried to control her, but she was ruined by your silly mother, you know, James. And as she got older she did just what she liked. I had said to your mother that Maria would get herself into trouble the way she was going."

Rose was being honest, I felt. Her bad mood made her less thoughtful in what she said. And what she was now saying was what I had always felt myself.

"So, what did they find out?" I asked. "Who last saw her?"

"I can't remember, James," she said, with a bit of irritation. "Some girlfriend she supposedly always came home on the train with. In those days only a few girls traveled into Newcastle, to St Cecilia's, from this far out. Everyone was asking the girlfriend what had happened, and all she was saying was that Maria had got off the train at her stop, Biraben, and they had waited together until she got on the train back to Fassiglen. She claimed that most afternoons Maria would ride to the next station, Biraben, where this girl, her best friend, got off. And then she would catch the train back to Fassiglen. Girls that age often do foolish things like that, James."

I was pleased to have what I had learned earlier from the newspapers confirmed.

"For the first few days I don't think they really believed she was gone. It's hard to believe someone has vanished. Your father nearly had a breakdown at the start; then he went very strange about her later. But you know that."

I left Rose not long after. Cicely was being loud and difficult, and Frank had still not come home.

I drove to Biraben train station, where Maria's school friend said she had last seen her. It was a small, modern, unmanned station that had obviously been rebuilt since her disappearance, and I walked dispiritedly up and down the two bare platforms. There was nothing on them but a few benches and a small closed-in shelter on each platform. One shelter held an automatic ticket machine, and I stood and looked at it, knowing no such thing had been there when Maria disappeared.

The two platforms were exposed on all sides; the land around was mostly cleared and old houses ran along a road fifty meters away. I had no idea what it had been like thirty years before. And if the girlfriend had seen Maria get on the train back to Fassiglen station, there were no secrets to be discovered at Biraben anyway.

I could easily imagine two schoolgirls sitting on one of the station benches together, talking, laughing, and giggling, like girls that age do, as they waited for the next train. It possibly explained too why I had the impression Maria had always arrived home late in the evenings, not long before our father. If she had regularly taken the train to Biraben and back, it would have added time to her journey home. I wondered how long. At least half an hour I'd have thought, but maybe longer.

My father was always home by about five thirty, and we had dinner at six. That was our family routine. My mother stayed home and she always had dinner on the table ready for us when he came home and had showered and changed out of his work clothes. Later, when my mother had cooked dinner for just the two of us, it had still always been on the table at six. I had a feeling she liked it that way and that perhaps it had been her routine more than his. I could remember vaguely that he and

Effie had eaten later, at seven or eight. Now he ate at five and moaned about how early the home served dinner, as well as complaining about the food.

If Biraben station held any secrets about Maria's disappearance, it wasn't going to share them with me. I left and made the drive into Fassiglen station. It was still not seven and I was grateful that daylight saving meant it was still light.

The railway line from Sydney to Newcastle had been completed in 1889. There had been a short period when travelers had to take a ferry across the Hawkesbury river, about midway, and rejoin the train on the other side. But that had been only a brief period. The forests of the nearby Watagans had provided the timber for sleepers, and Newcastle had been a coal town from the beginning. Everything needed for a major rail line had been readily available.

Unlike Biraben, Fassiglen station had been built in 1888, and the main building housing the ticket office was still the well-preserved Victorian brick one, built on the Sydney side of the line. The other platform was barer, with a long, modern steel and glass shelter and not much else except the stairs up to the walkway across the tracks to the main platform, and the lift—a recent addition.

On the Sydney side of the station, behind platform one, was the large car park, where I parked my car, and at the bottom of the steps from the station forecourt was the bus stop.

I vaguely remembered that when I was young there had been a much smaller car park and the road up past the station building and ticket office had been narrow with cars able to park along it. In the early seventies a branch line had run from Fassiglen to Moorebank on the edge of the lake.

The road in front of the main station building had since been widened and changed, and the car park had been moved and enlarged. I wished I could remember when that had happened. I could remember my dad picking my mother and me up on the old road just outside the station building after we had been into Newcastle for some reason. But the old road was now a bus turning circle.

I walked along the Sydney platform to the stairs, then up and over to the other platform. I looked up and down it and out past the fence and saw the bush start behind an area of compacted earth that sat behind the platform. There was a gate opening on to that side with a sign saying "disabled parking area, entrance via Treasor St." on it. I had never noticed it before and wondered if it had been there when Maria had gone missing. That was the platform she would have got off on when she had returned from Biraben. If she had come straight home she'd have got off on the main, Sydney, platform.

I wondered again what she had been like. Wondering what she might have been thinking about as she got off the train coming back from her friend's station. Maria must have been picked up by someone at the station, or on her walk home. It had been a good twenty-minute walk from the station to our house, but it was down a fairly busy road with houses on either side. And we were well known in the area.

I could imagine almost anything happening. I had no idea what had.

If I had learned anything so far that day it was that Maria had been more likely the spoiled and rather selfish girl I had always thought of her as, rather than the perfect young woman, generous and loved by all, that the papers had been full of.

CHAPTER 25

Before I left the station I had walked back over the overpass to the station building and went up to the ticket window and called out.

A young man with thinning red hair and wearing a railway uniform appeared and came up to the counter.

"Do you know when the old road along the front of the station was closed off?" I asked.

"Seventy-five, I think," he replied, obviously having been asked before. "They closed the Moorebank Line in 1974 and then they redid the car park."

Seventy-four, I thought, so it had been closed off after Maria had disappeared.

"And I was wondering if you can tell me if there has always been a gate on the other side of the station, onto the disabled parking area behind that platform?"

"As long as I've been here," he replied, "But no one uses it now. You used to get to it from Treasor Street. You kept going off the end of it. People use the car park and the lifts now. It's much easier for the oldies."

"Do you know if that entry was accessible in the early seventies?" I asked.

"Can't help you there, mate," he answered with a laughed. "I wasn't even born. What do you want to know for?"

"My sister disappeared from here back then."

"Oh, wow, you're the brother. Frank mentioned he knew you—and her. He wouldn't talk about it, though. Apparently he was on holidays when it happened."

I thanked him. Then I walked back over to the other platform, deciding I might as well look around. If Maria had met someone here, the bush was a nice quiet spot, and private. Even the dirt parking area was hidden from sight below the level of the platform.

I walked through the gate and down the ramp, which looked new. But the lifts that bypass the long staircases up to the flyover were recent, I reminded myself. Before they were installed, this would have been a necessary entry or exit point for anyone who had trouble climbing stairs.

I wandered across the dirt area and looked into the bush. It was thick and went off as far as I could see. I walked along the dirt track leading away from the parking area, and shortly the station had disappeared. I could have been in any bit of bush anywhere. I imagined it was an ideal place for a private rendezvous back in the less-tolerant early seventies. And that was when I got a whiff of something rotting.

Acquaintances who lived further down the hill from me had lost a dog not long before. A big Labrador. It had panicked at the sound of fireworks and disappeared. That had been a couple of weeks ago, but I knew they had searched the bush all round, looking for the body, as he had never come back or been seen by anyone. So now I went in search of the smell. It was a dead kangaroo, though. I hadn't realized they were still about the area, and it was sad that the first one I had seen for some years was a dead one.

I left it there and returned to the station. I had forgotten how much less developed the area had been back then. Thirty years before one side of the road between where we'd lived and Fassiglen station had been bush, and kangaroos had been frequent visitors to the area. Now it was taken up with a religious school and houses.

Now the bush was only in the valley on the other side of the rail line.

CHAPTER 26

Jennifer Toomey lived in a small apartment complex built right beside the lake. It was a few years old, but the property was definitely part of millionaire's row, with a good, wide, deep-water frontage and its own private jetty.

When I'd arrived, I had been annoyed that I'd had to drive some way along the street to find a parking spot. Cars were already parked along one side of the narrow road that ran past the complex. Now I knew why. I had walked down to the front of the building to check out the location and the view and discovered that a new and very expensive fifty-foot yacht was tied up to the jetty and a party was under way on board, with people spilling out and sitting on the jetty and on the cabin roof.

I had arrived back from Darwin a couple of years too late to be able to afford to buy a waterfront property. In the few years I had been gone prices had moved out of my reach, and lately they had surged ahead again on the back of the stock market boom. I knew that I would never be able to afford the waterfront however well I invested my money.

But I comforted myself by remembering the cold gales that roared across the lake at times, making it impossible to have a window open or sit outside. And also by thinking of the constant and often expensive maintenance required by buildings on the waterfront, because the lake is salt sea water, not fresh. And not only that, there were also the council rates, which had skyrocketed along with land prices.

In real estate they say that the three essentials are location, location, and location. Jennifer's apartment building, with its view of paradise, met all three requirements. In the evening light the lake, the boats moored nearby and those sailing for home, as well as the view of the opposite shoreline presented a beautifully peaceful panorama. The neighboring properties were set back on large treed blocks and didn't intrude at all. I enjoyed the scene in private for a few minutes as I walked along between the lake and the building. The postcard-perfect image was spoilt only by a chill in the evening air, created by the breeze coming in off the water.

I had arrived early, but not on purpose. Going anywhere alone, I always preferred to arrive a bit late and join a group of people already relaxed and chatting. But my nerves were on edge, and I hadn't been able to sit at home and wait any longer.

Having walked around the building, I returned to the main entrance and pressed Jennifer's buzzer. There was a camera looking at me, and Jennifer's voice saying "Hello, James, come on up" was accompanied by the electronic click of the door lock disengaging.

"Thanks," I said, probably to no one, as I turned the handle and walked inside, the door thumping closed behind me as I climbed the stairs.

The building was too small for a lift, and the two flights of stairs up to Jennifer's top-floor apartment were wide and shallow and an easy climb. No doubt if prices went up enough a lift would eventually be installed.

She was waiting at the door for me when I arrived and gave me a friendly kiss on the cheek, setting my mind at ease about whether I was still welcome.

"The others haven't arrived yet," she said. "You're early."

I mumbled something, but she didn't seem bothered and led me through a comfortable living room onto the veranda overlooking the lake.

"Wow," I said, without being able to stop myself.

"Impressed?" she asked, smiling.

"Yes. The view downstairs is great, but from here. Well, it's amazing."

"People don't realize we are built on a point here," she said, smiling happily.

I certainly hadn't. The view was not only ahead but also swept around to the sides into curving bays as well as overlooking the main channel in both directions for quite a distance. Several sailing boats moved across the view coming and going. And the shore opposite stretched out of sight in both directions. The tall apartments at Belmont were clearly visible, but from her veranda they looked picturesque.

There was the sound of a buzzer and Jennifer disappeared inside, while my nerves made me forget the view and swallow hard.

Jennifer's friend, Pat, and her husband were obviously pleasant people. Pat was small, attractive, and shy and shook hands gently and briefly while looking intently at me.

"I can't see a resemblance," Pat said as soon as we had been introduced. "You're both dark, but not much alike otherwise, I don't think."

"When I was young, we were very alike," I replied.

Pat opened her bag and took out an envelope. "I have had this in a drawer for years. I have had it copied for you, James."

I opened the envelope and inside was a photo of three girls standing in front of what looked like an old cinema. It was small, and it was a moment before I picked out Maria, standing on the left of the group of three teenagers. I pointed at my sister silently, and Pat nodded.

"Maria, of course. I was sure you'd recognize her. That's Jennifer in the center and me on the other side. It was taken in front of the old Tower Cinema in Newcastle. We were there to see *Change of Habit*, with Elvis Presley. My mother took us all. It was my birthday present. I was fifteen."

"Thank you," I said. "Thank you."

I hadn't looked at a picture of Maria in years, I realized, and in the one Pat had given me, the figures of the three teenagers in short skirts and tight sweaters were so small it was hard to see much detail at all.

Jennifer had Pat's husband, George, take charge of the drinks, while she disappeared behind the high bench separating the kitchen from the living area. She emerged with some platters and Pat hurried over to help her. I was left wanting to talk and stopped by courtesy. We all knew why we were there, and there was plenty of time. But I very much wanted to know what Pat knew, and I wanted to know it immediately.

It transpired that the yacht tied up to the jetty outside belonged to one of Jennifer's neighbors with whom she was having a running battle about car parking, and the early talk over dinner flowed freely on the horrors of parking and body corporates, or co-ops, as Jennifer informed us the American's called them.

"I was shocked when I read about Maria being found, James," Pat said. "I mean I had really forgotten all about it, which sounds awful, but there hadn't been anything to bring it back to mind for years."

"What my wife means," George said, "was that it was an awful experience when it happened, and she's tried to forget it."

"I can tell him, George," Pat said petulantly. "The police interviewed me at the time, you know. I was upset and I was also frightened and confused. At the start I was being loyal to Maria. Then later it was too late, I couldn't suddenly change my story. I had a long talk with a nice policewoman one day, and I so wanted to tell her the truth, but I just couldn't. It was ghastly. I was a mess." She stopped for a moment. "I have to confess, James, that there were several things I didn't tell them. But most of it wasn't really about that day itself. So it may have nothing to do with her disappearing," she reassured me, putting a hand out to touch mine briefly to help make the point. "It was about what had been going on before." She looked at her husband. "George says the police will want to know. But he says it's my choice if I go to them. George knows most of the local ones, fortunately."

"Never get involved with the police if you can avoid it," George said firmly. "But then I don't want to see a murderer going free either. And Pat has suffered a lot, worrying, because she didn't tell them everything back then. I don't want her to have it eating away at her any longer. But it's her decision."

"I have hardly heard anything about what is going on, except that they called my cousin," I said reassuringly. "Apparently they always do some sort of investigation when there is a suspicious death or murder involved, though in this case they don't seem to be in any hurry. But after all it was a long time ago, and whoever killed Maria is possibly dead now too."

"I just don't want Pat caught up in any sort of media circus. The police are bad enough. But what those journalists get up to sometimes is disgusting. They're like a herd of mindless elephants stampeding around after each other as soon as they smell a story. Working at the courthouse, I've seen it. They'll walk over anyone. And then they print mostly rubbish anyway, to make things sound more sensational then they are."

The media were obviously a hobbyhorse of George's, and he was getting quite irate just talking about them. I was being patient, but what I wanted to talk about was what Pat hadn't told the police or had lied about to them back in the beginning.

Fortunately Pat tapped her husband's arm and shut him up, "Now, now, George, it hasn't reached that stage yet." Then she turned her attention back to me. "Anyway, what James wants to know is what I didn't tell anyone." She hesitated nervously. "Maria had been seeing someone. I didn't know who. She never said a name or much else. She was very secretive about it, but she said things. So, I knew. But I don't think anyone else did really. Did you, Jennifer?"

"No. But I told James I had a feeling there was someone, someone she didn't want anyone to know about. Maybe a boyfriend a lot older than her."

"So, how did you know?" I asked Pat.

"I just knew. She was glowing and she said things. Not who, but a bit about what they had done, and she said things that made it clear she was having sex with whoever it was."

"What sort of things?" I asked, wondering if anything Pat thought she knew was just her imagination.

"About being touched. About the taste of cigarettes in someone's mouth. I was shocked. When I asked her what was going on, she just said that when I was a woman I would understand. And that being a woman was wonderful."

"So it wasn't a school friend?"

"St Cecilia's was a girls' school, James," Jennifer reminded me, smiling.

"No, it definitely wasn't one of the boys who we saw on the train or at events," Pat replied. "There was a signal they had, I am sure. But those last few days things were different. She was sad suddenly, though she had been excited and tense for ages before that. But it wasn't a bad things happening sad, just a lonely sort of sad, and she hardly talked. It was going to be her birthday soon, and the only thing she really talked about was a wonderful surprise that was happening that day, and she'd glow. And then she was gone.

"Now and then she used to ride with me to Biraben station, but not often. Then in the last week or so on about four or five occasions she didn't get off at Fassiglen station; instead she rode on to Biraben and got off with me and then she would wait and catch the first train back. A few months before she had asked me to say she was doing that every day, and I had agreed. And I had told a couple of people she was. She kept reminding me about it and I kept on saying it. In the end, I even told the police she had been going on to Biraben every day for ages. But she hadn't. She only did it occasionally, until that last week."

"Maria was getting home late for months before she went," I responded. "And I read about Biraben in the newspaper and thought that explained why. But you're saying that it was only occasional times when she did go on to your station with you. Do you have any idea what she did the other times?" I wanted to be sure I was clear.

"I knew she was seeing someone. At that age secrets like that seem romantic. And exciting. And sex seemed a lot more exciting in those days." Pat was starting to look upset. "Of course, secrets aren't romantic. I wondered even then if things would change if she found out she was pregnant. But she never said anything. In those days that was a disaster if you didn't get married, and your father was pushing her to go to teachers college."

"Allison told me a few days ago that my mother thought Maria was pregnant. But she didn't actually know, she only suspected it."

Pat dabbed at her eyes and nodded her head. "Maria was spoilt by your parents, but she thought she was being treated badly and was annoyed she was expected to make something of herself. There was a lot of pressure, but I think she hated the idea of teachers college. Of more study."

"So, what happened on the days she didn't go on to Biraben with you? Did you see anyone waiting for her?" I asked, wanting to stop her from moving on and desperately wanting to get inside Pat's head and see what she had seen back then. I had a sudden wave of certainty that Pat knew the whole answer to Maria's disappearance.

"Maria would press her face to the window, looking forward as we approached Fassiglen station, so she could see the station before we arrived. Then she would either get off the train or stay on. I asked her what was going on. What she was looking for, and she said "nothing," which was pretty obviously wrong. But all she said was, "it was nothing."

Anyway, after that I tried looking at the station too as we approached it, and I was pretty sure it was a car being there that made her go on. It was small and blue and would be parked right by the kerb near the end of the platform. At the side of the road by the station, near where the bus used to stop. They have changed it all since then. Now there is a big car park and a turning circle for the bus.

"Anyway, if the blue car was there, she went on, and if it wasn't, she got off. Then I didn't see the blue car again, but she didn't get off on a few days when there was a different car there, a red car. I thought he must have changed cars. Then there was no car there for a few days, I am sure, but she still didn't get off, which surprised me." She stopped and wiped her eyes.

"You have no idea how often I went over those last few days in my mind, after it happened. I could play them through in my head like a movie. I would wake up at night dreaming Maria had gone under the train's wheels and been squashed into nothing. It was awful."

Pat was now openly teary, and George had an arm around her shoulder, stroking her back. But he said nothing, and I was surprised.

"I'm sorry," Jennifer and I said together.

"I had no idea," Jennifer added. "But I didn't catch the same train home, we lived in Belmont then. I only saw Maria at school or if we went out together."

Pat shook her head and wiped her eyes dry. "It's good to talk about it. I haven't even told George everything before tonight."

"The last day or two she didn't look out of the window the same way as usual—for the first time—and I was surprised. Then that last day I saw the red car was there, and I expected her to stay on the train with me, but she seemed really shocked when she saw it and suddenly nervous and she got off in a rush. She had said she'd go on with me. And that was it. She was nervous and excited and she got off at Fassiglen. And I never saw her again."

"What sort of car was the red one?" I asked, doubting she would know.

"It was a Monaro," she said positively.

"You're sure?" I asked.

"Oh, yes. Definitely. It was a red Monaro. I knew them. It was glossy, and new. I thought those cars were wonderful. And it was there for a few days before she disappeared, when she stayed on to Biraben. We waited on the station for the return train, but she was quieter than usual. Then the next day it was there again she got off and disappeared."

"And the blue car?"

"I have no idea, I never really knew which cars were what."

"You don't have any idea whose car it was or who was in the car?" I asked. "You didn't see him anytime? And she never gave any hint?"

"No. I didn't see anyone, sorry—just the car. And I can't be completely sure that was why she went on or got off, anyway. It may have been something else I didn't notice, but I doubt it," she thought a while, "No, it had to be the car, or else it was an incredibly huge coincidence."

"You said you didn't know cars, so are you sure the red one was a Monaro?" I asked.

Pat hesitated. "Yes, definitely. My brother had a picture of a red Monaro up in his bedroom. It was a poster he had hanging over his bed. His aim in life was to own one. He never did, though. He died fighting in Vietnam. He never had a car at all; he never even had time to get a driver's license." She was openly crying again.

I felt awful. I felt a great compassion for her, for the losses she had suffered so far away in space, and now in time.

"I'm sorry, Pat, that this has brought that up," I said.

Pat brushed away the tears and asked for another drink, and George bit his lip. I wondered whether her husband was afraid she would now drink too much. Or if he was just concerned because he loved her, or was worried she would be weepy for the rest of the evening. I couldn't tell. But I respected him as a man who genuinely cared for his wife, and as they must have been married for well over twenty years, I also realized that they were still strongly connected and that it was a good marriage. He was a better and luckier man than I was.

George suddenly became funny and told a couple of stories about the magistrate's courts to lighten the atmosphere. He was a good storyteller and had access to some excellent material and soon had us all laughing, including Pat. Then he encouraged Pat to leave and quickly shuffled her out of the door.

"I'd forgotten about her brother," Jennifer said, as she closed the door behind them. "He was a lovely boy, I had quite a crush on him before he got called up. He was a conscript. The funeral was terrible."

We both sat there in our own thoughts for a few minutes. Young people don't die. That's the way we feel nowadays, I realized. But in the real world they do. And in the past they died often. I mentally shuddered for a moment, wondering what it must have been like if you had been in the generation of Australians who had lived through the First World War, when half the eligible men had gone to war and one in five had died. The horror of sitting around at a dinner party and reminiscing, with so many ghosts lying just below the surface.

And back then there were so many things for the people you'd loved and grown up with to die of. Tuberculosis, the war, influenza epidemics. But perhaps you never talked about them, I thought, or perhaps there were so many of them it had seemed natural and talking of them showed respect as much as an affirmation of their brief existence as gratitude for your own survival.

Life was too fragile, I suddenly thought, and I had a sudden urge, an overwhelming need, to join my body to another, to escape from the danger and loneliness of death. Hold it away.

I looked over at Jennifer, and she was flushed, her face smudged, and I knew I could comfort her, join my body to hers. That she wanted it too.

"How about we have a coffee in the lounge?" she asked.

"Fine," I murmured, and she moved into the kitchen and I sat on the sofa looking toward the nighttime lights of Belmont.

When she came back, she sat next to me, and I slipped an arm around her. She gave into me, the soft submission of a giving woman. And immediately I knew it was a mistake.

I made some apologies and left, kissing her good-bye with a deep physical regret.

As I drove away I was grateful for the information the evening had given me but confused about my own feelings.

I was soon diverting my thoughts by wondering how I could possibly find out more. There couldn't have been too many red Monaro's around the lake back then and it sounded like the kind of car Rocky could have had.

CHAPTER 27

I had wanted to ring Ray immediately and ask him whether Rocky ever had a red Monaro. But when I got home it was far too late to be ringing, and I knew I had to wait until morning.

I couldn't remember Rocky having a red Monaro, and I was sure I would have. But then again he may only have got it shortly before Maria disappeared. I vaguely remembered that Rocky often had a new car. There had been some talk about him buying them cheap, fixing them up, and selling them for a better price. Back when I was a kid it had sounded like the really clever sort of thing Rocky would do. The Holden Monaro was an icon of the seventies and I, like Pat's brother and every other boy back then, had ogled it at one time. I wondered if the police were able to check the ownership of cars back that far. I thought that nowadays they could run a search and find the details of every one of a particular car in the state, but I doubted they could look very far into the past.

"Do you know if Rocky had a red Monaro when Maria went missing?" I asked Ray when I finally caught him. "I know he had a lot of different cars, but I didn't see him that often and I don't remember a Monaro. I think I would have."

"A red Monaro? He had one for a while, but I can't remember when he got it. I think it came from some mate," he said. "It was after I met Dessi, but I started going out with her about the time your sister disappeared. So I doubt he had it when she went missing. But it was a long time ago, and I could have the timing wrong. He might have had it then. Is it important?"

I told him about Pat's story. "Oh, it doesn't sound like it was Rocky, James," Ray responded afterwards, sounding disappointed. "I'm sure he got the car from a mate who was going to jail in return for doing something for him. That was very like Rocky. Rocky had a lot of dodgy mates. He could have borrowed it sometimes before he actually got it, though, I suppose. But I don't see him heading up there every few days just to see a girl."

"Do you have any idea who the friend was?" I asked.

Ray laughed, "Sorry mate, I tried to avoid having anything to do with anyone he knew. All I know is the guy who owned it, or had it, anyway, needed a favor. Whether it was when your sister disappeared or a couple of years later I really don't know, and I am not asking Dessi. He didn't keep it that long, about six months maybe, he certainly didn't have it when he died."

My first thought had been, did Rocky have a Monaro? I hadn't really thought about anyone else, I was so caught up in the idea that Rocky had been involved with Maria's death. Apart from the sort of man he had been it was tidy. He was dead too. If he had murdered Maria then in a way he had been punished already.

125

CHAPTER 28

I came back to the present and saw Allison and Wolfy coming through the doors into the funeral chapel. She smiled at me from the entrance, and she and Wolfy walked toward me, as I walked toward them.

"Hello, James," she said and gave me a brief kiss on the cheek before pulling away. I wanted to hold on to her, have her beside me.

"Hello, Uncle James," Wolfy said, looking up with a big smile.

The first time he had come to my house with his mother I had been worried that what happened with Cicely would happen with him too. And it might have if Allison hadn't been who she was.

Wolfy saw the dogs outside and started to open the sliding glass doors. When the dogs ran up and fought to get in through the crack he backed off, frightened, which was natural really. But Alison rushed up and held his hand and opened the door quickly so the dogs dashed in, and past them, to jump on me. Wolfly had gone from fear to laughter as I disappeared under the pack, and Allison had joined him. A short while later he was outside throwing a ball for them, though they were not very interested in chasing it.

Allison stood at the window beside me, watching him. "You were always good with the dogs," she said. "You let them be dogs, but you do your best for them."

"You were good with them too; they never looked well groomed after you left."

"Maybe they need two parents."

"Kids frighten me. They are such a big responsibility, and it's so easy to make mistakes. Dogs are easy," I replied, as afraid as I ever had been of having children and making their lives miserable.

In the chapel, Rose appeared beside us. "I had heard you were back," she said to Allison as she stood there defensively beside me and showed her anger at Allison and Wolfy being there.

The last time Rose had seen us together had been years before, just before Allison had met her German and we had obviously not been getting along.

"Hello, Rose. How are Linda, and Cicely?" Allison asked.

"They are both very well," Rose replied sharply. "We are James's family now."

"I see someone I know, so I will catch up with you later, James," Allison said. "Nice to see you again, Rose." She turned and left with Wolfy's hand firmly in hers.

Rose turned to me, "Don't let yourself get hurt again, James. You have done very nicely without her all these years."

"Yes, I have, Rose." I said, smiling at her and seeing the fire in her eyes.

Part of me wanted Allison to come back and stand beside me as people arrived, but of course she couldn't. It would have been assuming too much and making a public statement about something we hadn't even discussed yet.

I knew that it was time we talked about it.

Since that first meeting at the lakeside café, my thoughts had been with Allison more than with Maria. I had been stunned to discover Allison had known about the skirt. I had briefly felt like killing her for knowing that.

"Was it Maria's?" Allison had asked me next, as If that would explain everything.

"What are you saying?" I asked her instead of just answering. Instead of telling her the truth.

"I am not saying anything James. I came back home one day, early, and I couldn't find you in the house, so I went out to the garage to see if your car was there. The door was partly open. I looked in and I saw you. You were standing in front of the old wardrobe at the back, looking at yourself in the mirror . . . with the skirt on." She paused and shrugged. "I had no idea what to say. I was horrified. I was young and naïve, James. I took it personally. But I have always wondered if that was the reason for a lot of our problems. That you needed to dress as a woman to enjoy sex."

"I never needed to dress up as a woman," I hissed back angrily, looking about and hoping no one in the café could hear her.

The conversation was worse than embarrassing. It was mortifying. When I was married I had rarely retreated to the garage and the escape and freedom I felt when dressing as Maria. I had never wanted anyone in my real world to know about what I did in Maria's clothes. It was private. Back then it had only been at rare times when I desperately needed it.

"It was nothing," I said. "Forget it. Things didn't work out, Allison. Maybe because I had issues I had to deal with. And I am not having this conversation here in public."

"Then I had better go," she said with a flash of anger, pushing her chair back.

"No," I said, grabbing her wrist, frightened she would disappear from my life again. "No," I said, "I don't want you going. Not like this," I added, surprised at how strongly I felt.

She stared at me challengingly for a few moments then softened, and I groped for an opening.

"Let's walk," I said, standing up, taking her hand, and pulling her up out of her seat.

The café we were in sat on the side of the road that ran along the lake from the Royal Motor Yacht Club to the boat yard. The lake was sparkling in the sunlight and the foreshore was almost deserted, it was far more private than the café. If she had to talk, we could do it there. The old Allison would have apologized and not said any more, but the new one was obviously more demanding. And I wanted her to like me.

"The clothes were Maria's," I said, having no idea how to explain myself, or what to say. I didn't want to have to justify myself.

"Ah." was all Allison said, and the silence dragged out until I had to speak.

I had no idea how best to tell my ex-wife, the woman I was again in love with, about the sexual illusions I had created as a teenager, had rarely used when married, but had returned to since we parted.

"My mother gave me a lot of negative ideas about sex when I was young. And I discovered one day that it was easier for me if I pretended I was Maria. I looked very like her at one time when I was young. My parents had thought she was perfect, but to me she was always very, very sexual for some reason. So it was OK to be her and want sex." I paused and turned to look at Allison. "Does that make any sense? I don't actually want to be a woman myself—"

"Oh, James," she said. "A couple of times I heard your mother in one of her moods. I wondered if she had been like that when you were younger and how bad it might have been, but—"

"She was worse, much worse than anything you ever heard. Day after day. And somehow I always believed Maria had been a bit of a tart."

"Did you know that your mother thought Maria was pregnant when she went missing?"

It took a few moments for what Allison had said to sink in. "She thought what?" I had said, stunned. "She always thought Maria was perfect. How could she—?"

"Think that Maria had been pregnant when she went missing? I doubt she made it up, as it made it worse for your mother that Maria hadn't told her. Your mother liked to imagine that she and Maria had some psychic bond, or at least the perfect mother daughter relationship, with no secrets. To think that

Maria had not told her that, and worse, that she had a boyfriend she had not told your mother about didn't fit in with that image. I think it made her feel very bitter and perhaps also very guilty."

Allison's words washed over me. "Maria pregnant?" I said, still trying to come to grips with that. "So she did have a boyfriend then." All the things I had felt about her and had been feeling guilty for thinking appeared to have been true. "Didn't my mother have any idea who she was seeing?" I asked, also hating my mother suddenly for her lies and deceit. "And how dare she abuse me the way she did. When Maria was doing whatever she liked and getting away with it, and still being treated like a princess," I said angrily.

"James. It was a long time ago."

"Feeling Maria was like that was what made it all work for me. I put on her clothes and looked like her and it was OK to want it. To do it. It had nothing to do with you, it started long before that," I said. "But it made it harder you trying so hard all the time. Wanting us to have sex all the time."

"It was hardly all the time James. Don't exaggerate, but I did get rather obsessed at one stage, I know," she said with a smile.

Her smile broke the tension.

"I needed time," I said.

"Do you still need to be her?"

"I don't know, but now it seems that I can't be," I replied, "Now that she is dead I feel ridiculous even thinking about it, and . . . and it makes me feel very uncomfortable thinking of her."

We talked about other things as we walked as far as the yacht club; then we turned back. I felt I could have walked all day with her, but her parents would be bringing her son, Wolfgang, home soon and she wanted to be there when they arrived. For the first time I wondered what he looked like, and what sort of child he was.

"You must bring him and come and see the house," I said, as we walked back to the café and our cars.

"I would like that," she answered. "I confess I drove past your house the other day to see it. It looks very nice."

"Not too modern?"

"No. It looks light and airy, almost as if it was floating among the trees."

I was surprisingly pleased that she liked it. It had been my dream house, never hers. I had been pleased in a way to be able to build it alone, without her practical mind making helpful suggestions and changes. It was all mine.

That first meeting seemed so long ago now, so much had happened since.

CHAPTER 29

After that first meeting I had gone home and wandered about restlessly. I was full of confusing desires and questions. I wanted Allison as much as I ever had. There had obviously always been more there between us than just my desperate desire for a family.

I was also angry with my mother, because apart from Allison, she didn't seem to have told anyone, including the police, that she had believed Maria was pregnant. Knowing that might have made a big difference back in the beginning. They would have looked very hard for the boyfriend, I had no doubt She was a teenage girl and at that time getting a girl pregnant had carried far more baggage than it did now. It was a motive for a lot of things, including murder.

Pat's lies would also have helped to divert the police from the hunt for a boyfriend.

But now I felt physically uncomfortable too. My conversation with Allison had brought to the surface my growing discomfort with the fantasy I had been playing out in different ways for so many years. The many variations of me hiding behind Maria and of me becoming her. She was dead, and I wanted the rest to die with her.

I went into the spare room and looked at the wardrobe doors for a few minutes before I opened them. Inside were my rarely worn coats and jackets and the unwanted clothes that were too good to throw out. And at the bottom and on the top shelf were the usual suitcases and bags you expect to find in a wardrobe. Along with some cardboard boxes. The usual sort of stuff.

But the sight of those boxes sent a rush of blood to my head. I hadn't opened them since they had been moved into my new house. I had packed them and taped them up just before I went to Darwin over twenty years before. I had wanted to be sure that what was inside them would be safe and hidden in case I returned. Though when I had left, I had thought with relief that I would never return to my mother's house.

The boxes had still been there when I cleaned out the garage after her death. As I knew they were. Once I had returned from Darwin I had occasionally felt compelled to check that they were safe.

It was the money I had inherited from my mother after the sale of her house that had enabled me to build my new house just as I wanted it. I had a good job, but even so, for anyone living alone on one salary it would have been impossible to afford the mortgage I would have needed for what I really wanted. Even when Allison and I were married it would have been hard.

Moving out of my old house and seeing it pulled down had been good for me. The old house had been full of Allison, the failure that had been our marriage, and my own inadequacies. The new house was an affirmation of my ability to create something beautiful and lasting. To be open to the wide views of the surrounding hills and the lake had felt like opening myself up to the world too. With its large glass doors and veranda, it let in fresh air and that had also in some way invigorated and refreshed me mentally. But some things hadn't changed.

I took down the three boxes and put them on the bed, but I couldn't bring myself to open them. They represented a powerful part of my life. My past. They represented my struggle to grow up. They represented the strange emotional bond I had imagined I'd had with my sister. A bond that had allowed me to cast off the guilt and self loathing I had felt when I didn't have her to hide behind.

I took them outside and burned them unopened.

* * * *

A week before the funeral I fucked her.

No. A week before Maria's funeral I made love to my ex-wife, Allison. In a haze of lust. I had found the familiarity of her shape and desires, and also discovered the changes in her. The changes brought to her body and mind, by time, another man, and a child.

I had broken myself against her. Like some wave crashing against a rocky shore. But I had also discovered something I hadn't known I needed to discover.

CHAPTER 30

There was a lull in the arrivals, and I looked about the chapel, wondering at the reasons people were there and wondering too how I would feel if somewhere in that crowd was the person who had killed my sister. It had happened thirty years ago, so whoever it was had to be in their late forties at least, as old as one of her school friends would be. I glimpsed Jennifer talking to two other women who were already seated a few rows from the front. A woman or a man. A man? Her lover perhaps?

Family, friends, or lovers I thought again. Not a woman. Definitely not a woman everyone would say. A man.

Linda came inside off the veranda with Cicely. There was still no sign of Frank, and Rose was roaming about looking as if she was busy catching up with friends.

"When is Frank coming?" I asked.

"I'm not sure. There is something going on with him and mum. Mum had to take Cicely shopping with her yesterday. She wanted me to go over and mind her, but I was at work. He wasn't at home when I went there to pick them up to come here."

"He hasn't run off and left her, has he?" I asked, jokingly.

"God no. No, I saw him there yesterday evening. I went over to see if Mum was all right, and he was there as usual. But she was in a weird mood. After I spoke to you the other night I thought a lot about him and how he has had a rather sad life. He got a fancy car at one time and Mum went berserk. Poor guy couldn't even enjoy himself a bit. She made him sell it and buy a Ford station wagon. I can remember being really disappointed, because all my friends in the street envied me riding around in the fancy red car he had."

"What kind of car?"

"I have no idea. I'll see you after," she said and moved off.

My dad had still not arrived. I was not surprised.

The inside seats had filled up and new arrivals were having to stand about outside.

I found Allison and murmured to her; then I left.

For a few days I had brooded on what Pat had said, then I had rung Inspector Wright and passed on most of it.

"Ah, I hope you aren't playing detective, Mr. Morgan. We are looking into things, and it's often best that fewer people know certain things. Please don't tell anyone what you have told me. You haven't, have you?"

"No, no," I said guiltily, "I needed to know more about her, though. It's been a long time."

"Yes, it has, I can understand that."

Then I had rung my father and asked if Frank had ever worked for Nick.

When I arrived at Rose and Frank's house Frank was not there and his car was gone too. I returned to the chapel before the funeral was over to find my father and Frank standing on the veranda, looking in.

"You came," I said to my father, both confused and pleased that he was there.

"Frank bring me," he said. "Where you been? You should be inside. Go, go."

"You should be inside too, Dad."

"No. I come; that is enough."

"Frank, thanks," I said, but he didn't look at me. It was obvious neither of them wanted to talk, so I moved to the door and looked in but didn't want to disturb the crowd by going back to my seat inside.

As the funeral service ended, I looked around for my father and saw that he and Frank were not alone anymore. There were two men and a woman in suits with them.

I didn't know them, but most of those there were strangers and I went in to join Allison and Wolfy. As we left the chapel together, I saw Rose being taken aside by the three strangers in suits and Frank leading Linda and Cicely off to one side, and I stood there transfixed while I watched my father and Frank looking on as Rose was being guided away from the crowd to a car parked in the space reserved for the undertaker.

"What. . . ?" Allison pulled at my arm.

"Nothing, don't worry about it; I'll tell you later." I said.

My father came over. "Go, go, James. Supper; go have something. I come with you. He wanted to marry her. He swears it." he stopped and wrung his hands, his face creased as if he might cry. "She was not such a bad girl."

"What's happening," Allison asked. "Why are they taking Rose away?"

CHAPTER 31

Maria had paid for her own funeral, and I had organized the best. I had not wanted any money to be left afterwards. It was hers, and I had thought too many things that had been unkind because of it. The chapel was well stocked with flowers, her coffin was a fine polished timber one with brass handles, and even what she wore was expensive. There had been no old clothes for her to wear. Everything of my sister's was gone. What she wore now I had bought new, and even though there was little but a skeleton inside her coffin, she was dressed in something I hoped she would have liked. And there was supper after the service and her burial. She was to be buried again, but this time permanently, next to our mother, where we would all know where she was.

Later I made love to Allison in the fading light of evening, possessing her as she wrapped her thighs about me and gave small high-pitched cries. She was like some bird, straining to reach that point in the infinite distance that was what life was all about.

Somewhere in my head a voice was telling me this—that the burning heat and need I felt, was what caused evil and wickedness. But another part of me instinctively knew this was what I needed, what Allison needed, what fed the endless cycle of life. And that it was good.

I knew that I would probably always be confused.

THE BEGINNING

Maria hadn't expected to see the red Monaro there. Frank was supposed to be away for another day, then he'd get a day at home before he went off again. She missed him badly. He was driving for her dad's brother, Nick, making extra money doing the Broken Hill run for a couple of weeks. Frank didn't want them to be dependant on her money when they took the Monaro and left Moorebank behind.

But the car was there and she suddenly was worried something may have happened to him or . . . her heart flipped, had he missed her so much he'd driven all night to come back to her early?

She had told Pat she'd ride on to Biraben with her, but instead she got off the train at Fassiglen, having to see Frank and know what had happened.

When she got to the car, though, it was Rose sitting in the driver's seat, with the window down. "Get in, Maria, I'll drive you home," she said.

It was strange to see Rose in the car, but Maria was not really thinking. Her thighs had got hot and her mind fuzzy at the thought of Frank unexpectedly being there, and she got in.

"Thanks, Rose. How come you came? Is everything OK?" She wondered vaguely if something had happened at home, but it was not an important thought.

"Yes, something is wrong," Rose said as she gunned the motor. "You are wrong. You leave my husband alone, you tart, or I'll make your life hell."

It registered that Rose was angry and knew about them, and Maria wasn't sure what to do. The car was going fast and she was caught by surprise.

"What do you mean, Rose? There's nothing between Frank and me. What an idea. He's so old," she said, trying to make it sound bad, whereas his age was part of what excited her, his experience and the maturity. He was twenty-four, and she was only seventeen.

"Liar," Rose barked. "I saw you. How stupid do you think I am? I knew he was up to something. Do you think you are the first? He chases anything. I followed him and saw you go off together on the other side of the station. He said he was up the pub. Well, that is going to stop, I can tell you. You are not going to see him again. I'll tell your father, and I will beat the shit out of you if you come near him again."

Maria felt like laughing. Who did this woman think she was? "Frank loves me, not you," she said, thinking that would say it all.

"Loves you? Ha, he loves anything in a skirt, or out of it. You aren't the first, or the last."

"He loves me," Maria repeated vehemently. "He's going to leave you for me. He's had enough of you. He never loved you. He only married you because you were pregnant. I am the one he loves and wants to be with."

Rose laughed a false "ha ha ha." Then she said, "You stupid girl. He doesn't love you."

"Oh, really? We are going to Brisbane. As soon as I turn eighteen, we are out of here. I have Gran's money, and he is driving for Uncle Nick to make extra. And his brother, Reg, has got a job lined up for him in Brisbane."

Maria felt a bit guilty about saying so much, but it was all true. And it was too late; it was out.

"And I am pregnant and we'll be in Brisbane as Mr. and Mrs. Clarke before anyone knows I am."

Rose laughed again but a real laugh this time. "It's not his. I've tried to have his kid for four years, and all I have got is one that is never going to grow up. It's not Frank's; it belongs to whoever else you've been sleeping with."

"I was a virgin, Rose," Marie responded angrily. "A virgin when Frank and I made love the first time." She had the high ground, she knew. It was Frank's.

"A virgin? Ha."

"Yes, Rose, a virgin. I know who the father of my child is, and it's Frank. We are in love, and we are getting out of this place and starting a new life together."

She had said it all now, there were no more secrets. Rose was quiet, and Maria looked at her. Rose's face was red. She was gripping the steering wheel of the Monaro with white-knuckled hands as she skidded around a corner and onto one of the tracks that ran into the bush between the station and Maria's home.

"Let me out, Rose," Maria said, worrying that Frank would be annoyed she had told Rose everything, even that she was pregnant, which he didn't know yet, and not wanting to continue the argument. "I will walk home."

Maria didn't feel unsafe. She had always got her own way whatever arguments there had been in her life. Rose was nothing but an inconvenience to her.

Then Rose reached her hand over and grabbed Marie by the throat, and, digging in her long nails, she gripped the soft neck hard and shook. The shock took a moment to get over. Then Maria slapped at Rose, trying to get her to let go, and screamed. Rose took her other hand off the steering wheel and grasped Maria's throat with both hands. She flung her body over Marie's, her face twisted with rage and her squeezing hands shaking, as the red Monaro slid off the track into some undergrowth and stopped.

The raging in Rose's mind eventually quieted and her fingers slowly uncurled from the neck they were wrapped about. Maria was silent at last and always would be now.

It was Frank's fault. All of it. Baby Cicely and her problems, this stupid girl, Maria, who was now lying dead in the car with her. Everything. He'd have to help her sort it out.

Outside the car it was quiet, and she dragged Maria's body back to the boot and after a struggle got her inside. No one had seen them she was sure and she got in and drove the car back onto the track and out of the bush.

When she got home she waited for Frank's nightly call. She'd agreed to him doing the extra work, foolishly thinking the money was for them, but she'd agreed only as long as he called her every night when he stopped. He'd have to help her sort it out. It was all his fault. The girls needed their mother. He'd understand that.

Stephen Bush

Stephen lives on the east coast of Australia, not far from Sydney. He works in publishing and writes, and his writing has been published often under other names. He regularly writes about dogs and runs training courses. Prior to moving to the east coast he lived in northern Australia and worked as an accountant. He likes the wide-open spaces. He also has too many dogs living in his house. But he loves them all.

Cyberworld Publishing
for
Murder & Mysteries

Stephen Bush
My Sister's Funeral

Olivia Stowe
THE CHARLOTTE DIAMOND MYSTERY SERIES
By The Howling
Retired with Prejudice
Coast to Coast
An Inconvenient Death

Gina Drew
THE KONIOTIS MYSTERIES
(Each book in this series stands alone, but they are also all connected and form the different parts of one story.)
Laughter's Echo
Salted Away
Mouflon Brigade
Amathus Armageddon
Bogus Bills
Homewrecker